The Healing Hills

By
Ruth Kyser

Copyright © 2014 by Ruth Kyser.

All rights reserved worldwide.

No part of this publication may be reproduced, stored in a retrieval system, or transmitted in any form or by any means— electronic, mechanical, photocopy, recording, or any other— without the prior permission of the author.

Scripture quotations are taken from the King James Version of the Bible.

This book is a work of fiction. Names, characters, places, and incidents are either products of the author's imagination or used fictitiously. Any similarity to actual people, organizations, and/or events are purely coincidental.

ISBN-13: 978-1502998644

ISBN-10: 1502998645

Dedicated to my sister, Millie, who recently reminded me of my love for the Smokies.

OTHER BOOKS BY RUTH KYSER:

"The Dove & The Raven –

A Christian Historical Romance"

"Endless Season"

"True Cover"

"Bluecreek Ranch" (Book 2 in "True Cover" series)

"Second Chances" (Book 3 in "True Cover" series)

"The Whispering Sentinel"

Author's Note:

I first saw Cades Cove in 1973. My sister and I visited the area, and I was completely unprepared for the feelings that would rush over me at my first glimpse of this magical place. I've never been able to find another spot in the world that rivals the beauty of the Great Smoky Mountain National Park (although I have to admit I haven't traveled everywhere).

My husband and I were fortunate enough to return to the area this past spring, and the journey brought back so many memories to me of that wonderful vacation when I was a young woman—filled with lofty hopes and dreams. Like Carrie in this book, the first time I got out of the car and took a breath of the fresh mountain air, I felt like I'd come home.

During my recent visit to the area I discovered there were, of course, many changes. A lot of the highways we now use weren't totally constructed back then. Instead, we traversed the area on two-lane roads that twisted and turned through the hills. Instead of wide four or six-lane highways, you crept along on roads over rickety narrow bridges that spanned the many rivers and creeks.

I was also shocked by the amount of traffic traversing through the Cove daily. When I first saw Cades Cove in 1973, there were still a few folks living in houses on the property—acting as caretakers of the land and livestock. We also didn't have the beautifully paved road to drive on through the Cove. The Loop Road was there, but you often had to drive through the rushing water of streams and creeks. Now I can only think of one spot on the Loop Road where you actually drive through the water from a creek—and I'm guessing in late summer, that water isn't even there.

What astonished me more than anything though was the vandalism I saw in the old historic cabins. The sight of people's names and other not-so-nice-things carved into the walls and wooden mantel inside the Henry Whitehead cabin just about broke my heart. I am unable to understand why anyone would want to destroy anything so historic and precious. What the people who do these things don't understand is, once the damage is done, it's done. There's no way to fix it. When I first saw the cabins of Cades Cove, they were still relatively untouched by vandals, and it was easy to envision what it must have been like to live in that area back in the 1800's—even into the early 1900's. For someone who loves history as much as I do, it was an awesome experience.

It's still an awesome experience.

I pray all of you who read this book can someday experience the beauty and peace of Cades Cove for yourself. If you do go though, I would ask that you remember and respect the people that came before you—those pioneers who built the cabins and barns, and farmed those fields all around the valley. Especially remember that the bear, wild turkeys, deer, and foxes are not there for your entertainment. The Cove is not a zoo. Cades Cove and the mountains and woods surrounding the Cove are their home. Watch them living in their natural habitat—at a distance, please.

Enjoy the beauty and peace of God's creation all around you, have respect for those who came before you in that marvelous place, and help to save it for future generations.

In Christ's Love,

Ruth Kyser

"I will lift up mine eyes unto the hills,

from whence cometh my help."

--Psalm 121:1

CHAPTER 1

*A*fter dragging her out of her bed in the darkness, the man straddled her body, holding her down on the floor with his left hand braced on her right shoulder and ripping at her nightgown with his other hand. She struggled and fought him with her legs, hands and fists, and screamed out in terror. He slapped her in the face, and the punch he landed on her jaw with his balled up fist made her senses reel. He beat on her body a couple more times with the same fist before his left hand clamped down over her nose and mouth to stop her from screaming. His hand greatly limited her ability to breathe, and while she struggled to get oxygen into her burning lungs, she prayed she would lose consciousness before the man was able to complete the act she knew was planned. She saw him pull out a knife and felt the coldness of the blade as he held it to her neck. Her time was up.

"God help me," she prayed silently. "Somebody, please help."

Carrie Montgomery gasped as her mind struggled to release itself from the nightmare that had haunted her sleep for months. Some would say it was just a bad dream, but to her it was so much more; she had lived it. She sat up in her bed and gulped in deep breaths of air, then swung her legs over the edge of the bed and dropped her head into her hands, flexing and rubbing her jaw with her right hand. He had almost broken her jaw with that first punch, and she had worn the bruises of the beating on her face and body for many weeks. After the man responsible for stalking her and then attacking her almost a year earlier had been caught and sentenced to twenty years in jail, she had prayed the bad dreams would cease, but she was still having them several times a week.

Would she ever feel safe again?

A glance at the alarm clock on her bedside stand told her it was only six-thirty in the morning. There was no need for her to get up so early, but after having the recurring nightmare, she was positive there would be no going back to sleep.

Carrie took a deep breath and exhaled it, then stood up and headed to her bathroom for a quick shower. She might as well get her day underway.

Fifteen minutes later Carrie was dressed, and had plaited her long, blond hair into a single braid. Dressed in casual jeans and her favorite Tennessee Volunteer tee shirt, she headed toward the aroma of coffee wafting from the direction of the apartment's kitchen. She found her best friend and roommate, Ashlynn Connors, seated at the small kitchen table, nibbling at a slice of toast, and sipping her mug of coffee. Carrie saw the surprise on her face as she looked in her direction.

"Why are up so early, Carrie? You're supposed to be on vacation, remember?"

Carrie grabbed a clean mug from the cupboard and poured herself a cup of the steaming brew, inhaling the aroma and feeling extra thankful this morning for things like strong cups of coffee. What with staying up late the night before packing for her trip, it had been a short night.

"It's not really a vacation, Ash. Remember?"

Her friend frowned and turned her attention back to the last bit of toast on her plate. "I remember. It just sounds so much better than saying you're on a forced medical leave."

Pulling out a chair, Carrie grimaced and took a seat across from her friend. After having several panic attacks and meltdowns in a classroom filled with second graders, the school administration had reluctantly made the decision she needed to take some time off, and she couldn't argue with them. She'd gone through months of therapy after the attack and she thought she had been making progress. So, why was she falling apart now?

"I think the term 'mental health leave' would be more appropriate," she finally mumbled.

Ashlynn looked at her over the rim of her mug. "After what you went through, Carrie, you deserve some time off, even if it is forced." She took a sip of her coffee and put the mug back down on the table. "Besides, how long has it been since you've been to Tennessee to visit your aunt?"

Carrie felt her lips curve up in a little smile at the mention of her great-aunt. "About fifteen years, I think."

Happy childhood memories swept through her mind as treasured recollections of sunny summer days spent on her aunt's and uncle's farm were recalled. If only going back to the mountains would erase all that had happened to her in the last fifteen years—although she had to admit, not all of those years had been bad. Most of the time, she was fairly happy with her life. She'd graduated from college, landed a job she loved as an elementary school teacher, and made some terrific friends.

She'd even had a serious boyfriend—for a while—until the attack had taken Sean from her too. At the thought of how Sean had dumped her, she grabbed a glazed donut from the box on the table and gobbled it down—even though she knew it wasn't good for her, and then swallowed the last of her tepid coffee.

She stood and left the kitchen, giving a little wave to Ashlynn as she departed. There was no sense stalling; she might as well finish packing and get on the road. It wouldn't be long anyway and Ashlynn would be leaving for her teaching job at the school, and Carrie didn't want to be left in the apartment alone any longer than necessary. Since the attack, it had been difficult for her to feel safe anywhere. They had talked about finding someplace else to live, but even with their pooled resources, they couldn't afford to move right now.

No; it was best she just get on with her life and try to put what happened behind her. Unfortunately though, because of what the psychologist had called her 'stressed mental state', she'd been told she couldn't go back to her teaching job until the next school year in September—at the soonest. That same psychologist had told her it would do her good to spend some time away from the city—somewhere with family—maybe in the country would be best. She had orders to continue her therapy sessions during the summer, and would have to have clearance to return to the classroom in the fall.

Hopefully that wouldn't be a problem.

Carrie had originally thought about going to Charlotte, North Carolina to visit her parents, but then her mom had suggested visiting Carrie's great aunt in southeastern Tennessee instead; someplace she hadn't been in years. Her mom passed the word along that Aunt Myrtle would love to see her, and Carrie decided it couldn't hurt to get away from everything and everyone in her life in Lexington for a while. There were too many painful memories here.

So, she'd reluctantly agreed, seeing it as a way to escape. Maybe if she wasn't here in Lexington for a while...maybe she'd be able to forget what had happened to her here. At least that was what she was hoping.

∧∧∧∧∧

Driving down the two-lane curvy road, with the waters of a rushing river on one side and the steep rocky sides of the mountains on the other, Carrie took in the scenery around her and smiled. As she relished in the feeling of the fresh mountain air sweeping through the open car windows, she was instantly transported back to her childhood—to a time when the arrival of summer meant a trip to the hills of Tennessee for a visit. It had been far too long since she'd been here.

Seeing the familiar mountains around her, it almost felt like she had come home.

She glanced over at the clock on the car's dashboard long enough to see it was almost noon. Unfortunately, she hadn't left Lexington as early as she would have liked due to a bunch of errands, including gassing up the car. She'd also had to drop by the school long enough to visit the administrative building and sign some papers. Because of all the errands, it had been later than she'd planned before she'd been able to leave the southern suburbs of Lexington and catch I-75 to head south. Carrie had enjoyed the drive through the rolling hills of Kentucky. The grass was just beginning to show shades of green, and she gazed out her car window to see horses gracefully grazing in pastures surrounded by miles and mile of bright white painted fences. Horse country.

She hated having to leave her classroom and her students in charge of a sub, but hopefully she'd be able to come back to Lexington in the fall and resume her teaching job again—as long as the school psychologist gave her the go ahead. At least, that is what they had told her and she really hoped they weren't lying to her. She hadn't even had an opportunity to say goodbye to her students.

Now she was here in the small town of her memories. Noon probably wasn't the best time to arrive at her aunt's restaurant, but she had no choice but to go there first. Aunt Myrtle was in possession of the key to her family's old cabin where Carrie was staying.

She drove slowly across what looked to be a new bridge that spanned the Little River and headed toward her aunt's restaurant on the other side of town. The small town of five hundred people didn't look like it had changed much over the years. There were still two churches, several restaurants, and a couple of motels and gas stations. Most of the tourists that came to visit the Smoky Mountains weren't looking for the peace and quiet they would find here in this small town. Gatlinburg, Sevierville, Pigeon Forge, and Maryville received most of the tourists. But fortunately, because of the town's proximity to the Smoky Mountains National Park and Cades Cove, there were still enough visitors to the area who wanted a quieter, more peaceful experience that the small businesses in town were able to stay open.

The building that housed *Meyers Place*, her aunt's restaurant, looked much the same as it had fifteen years earlier. The one story structure had a covered porch running the full length of the front, and boasted a green metal roof and bright red shutters at all the windows. The large sign assured 'good home cookin', and from what Carrie remembered, her aunt had always kept that promise.

Carrie pulled off the main road and drove into the gravel parking lot and parked in a spot away from the building, leaving the prime spots for the restaurant's patrons; although she was planning to eat her lunch here. Her mouth watered just at the thought of the good food she knew awaited her inside the restaurant.

She opened her car door and stepped out and took a deep breath of the fresh mountain air. It was a sunny day in late April, and the warmth of the sun felt good on her back, but the air around her still held the fresh coolness of the mountain air. Carrie stood for a moment and slowly turned in a circle as her eyes took in the vista of the mountains all around her. This small town was nestled in a valley of the Smokies, and the rolling hills surrounding her had areas that were almost lavender and white with the hues of the blossoming red bud trees and the flowering dogwoods. She knew it wouldn't be long and the mountain laurel and rhododendrons would add their variety of color to the hillsides.

She felt some of the tenseness of the past months fall from her shoulders as she turned and headed toward the restaurant. The sound of the bell clanging above the door brought a smile to her face as she entered the building. To the right was a counter with a cash register and a rack of postcards, and booths and tables and chairs sat on her left. It looked much the same as it had the last time she had seen it. Carrie had no more than cleared the doorway when she heard a familiar voice call out.

"There's my girl!" Her Aunt Myrtie, more gray and wrinkled that fifteen years earlier, rushed from behind the counter and enveloped her in a hug that took Carrie back to her childhood. Aunt Myrtie smelled like lilacs, French fries, and onions. She smelled like home.

Carrie's stomach growled in response and she heard her aunt's chuckle as she released her from her hug.

"Carolyn Elizabeth Montgomery, it has been FAR too long, since you have graced us with your presence. If your mom hadn't sent me photos of you over the years, I never would have recognized you."

Her aunt's voice was firm, but the smile on her face told Carrie how much love was behind the words. Aunt Myrtie pulled her back into a hug.

"I was so upset when your mom called and told me what happened to you," she spoke quietly into Carrie's ear.

"What's this world acomin' to? Well," her aunt stated as she pulled away again. "Sit yourself down at this table here and we're going to get you some lunch."

Carrie felt herself being tugged toward a small table and chair in the corner nearest the counter and gratefully took a seat. Her aunt sat down across the table from her, and looked at her expectantly.

"What sounds good to you for lunch, Carrie girl?"

She grinned at her aunt and shook her head. "Aunt Myrtie, I don't even know what's on the menu anymore. How about a burger and fries? That's always good."

Aunt Myrtie chuckled and stood from the table, patting Carrie on the shoulder as she stood next to her. "And how about a piece of my cherry pie for dessert?"

Carrie grinned up at her aunt. "You remember."

"Of course!" her aunt stated as she strode in the direction of the kitchen.

After Aunt Myrtie left her table, Carrie spent some time gazing around the small restaurant at the other patrons. Most of them looked like they could be locals; there were a couple of older gentlemen wearing bib overalls sitting in the far booth, sipping on coffee and finishing off slices of pie; a young couple sat in another booth, and an older woman sat at one of the tables with two pre-teens. There was a man in a business suit at small table, eating alone; Carrie was fairly sure he wasn't a local. And there was an older couple who looked like they were traveling through the area also. Carrie noticed they were studying a map on the table in front of them, so it was obvious they were not from around there.

Then her gaze turned to the décor of the restaurant. Aunt Myrtie had always taken pride in the neatness and cleanliness of the place, and it was obvious that hadn't changed over the years. Bright curtains hung at the spotless windows, and the walls looked like they were freshly painted a creamy off-white. And the floor—which was still the old original black and white checked tiles—had enough wax on them, they shone. Framed paintings depicting various scenes of the local countryside and historic buildings decorated most of the walls.

Carrie turned a little in her seat so she could better see one of the paintings hanging on the wall closest to her table. It was an oil painting of what she knew to be a cabin out at Cades Cove. She struggled to remember which one. Was it the John Oliver cabin, or the Elijah Oliver cabin? It had been so long since she had been out there, she couldn't remember. Either way, the painting was beautiful, with the low branches of a dogwood appearing in the picture just in front of the cabin. Sunlight filtered down through the trees, giving the whole area an almost heavenly glow. It looked so peaceful, and gazing at the painting gave Carrie a sense of contentment. She rose a little from her chair and tried to make out the tiny signature in the left corner. There was what looked like an "M" or maybe it was an "N", and was the last name Jones, or maybe Johnson?

She sat back down in her chair with a plop as her aunt placed a plate of hot food in front of her, along with a frosty glass of cola and a bottle of catsup. Carrie grinned as she saw the food. She was hungrier than she'd thought and it smelled heavenly.

"Thank you, Aunt Myrtie. This looks great!"

She felt her aunt's eyes rest on her a moment, then move to the painting Carrie had been studying. "Isn't it pretty? That painting there was done by Neil Johnston, a local artist." She gestured with her right hand in the direction of the rest of the restaurant. "All these were done by him. He's got a gallery at the other end of town you'll have to check out while you're here. He's also a big time photographer—even sells some of his stuff to national magazines, and he's done some sculptures too. The town's real proud of him."

Carrie shook her head. "I'm not in the market for paintings, Aunt Myrtie." She looked back up at the one on the wall next to her. "Although this is really nice. Maybe I'll visit the shop while I'm here. We'll see."

Aunt Myrtie touched her lightly on the shoulder. "Well, I'll let you eat your meal in peace and check back with you later. I need to get back to work anyway. You just let me know if you need anything else, sweetie. Okay? I'm so glad you're here. Now you just take your time and enjoy your food."

Carrie didn't hesitate to dig into the burger, savoring the taste of what she knew was locally raised beef. After she'd eaten most of the sandwich and half of the fries, she finally took time to watch her aunt in action. The lunch crowd had thinned out and there were now only a few stragglers left in the restaurant, finishing their meals or nursing their mugs of coffee. Since the noon rush was over, Aunt Myrtie sat on a stool behind the counter and directed two young women who were obviously waitressing for her on what to do next. She called one of them out of the kitchen with a large plastic tub to bus tables, and sent the other one out onto the floor with two pots of hot coffee to do refills. All this while making change for those customers ready to pay their bill.

Carrie shook her head. Her Aunt Myrtie was amazing.

Myrtle Meyers was really Carrie's great aunt—her mom's aunt, and the youngest sister of Carrie's grandmother. Myrtle was the last living member of that generation of the family, and Carrie knew she had to be in her early seventies. She sure didn't look it though. When she turned her hazel eyes on you, they were sharp and clear, and even though she wore glasses, those eyes took in everything around her. She kept her graying and wavy hair cut about chin length, and the wrinkles on her face were few. Aunt Myrtie had always been a classy dresser too. Today she was wearing black dress slacks and an aqua colored embroidered caftan top, covered with a freshly washed and bleached white apron emblazoned with the *Meyers Place* logo. Silver stud earrings sparkled in her ear lobes, and a silver brooch in the shape of a butterfly was pinned at her shoulder.

Aunt Myrtle was a widow, having lost her husband, Jasper Meyers, the summer Carrie was last here. He had been killed unexpectedly in a car accident one night coming home from town. Aunt Myrtie had already owned the restaurant, so she had simply picked up the pieces of her life and continued on, and Carrie had always admired her aunt for her get-it-done attitude.

Myrtie had two sons, Ralph and Walter, who both lived in Nashville, Tennessee with their wives and children. Carrie didn't know how often either of them made it home to visit their mom, but from what she could remember, they had seemingly turned their back on life here in the small town of their childhood. It made Carrie sad to think they didn't appreciate their mother as much as they should.

By the time Aunt Myrtie returned to Carrie's table with a huge slice of cherry pie, topped with a generous mound of vanilla ice cream, she had finished off all of her lunch except for a few French fries. She groaned as her aunt placed the plate with pie on the table with one hand and picked up the dirty dishes with the other.

"Aunt Myrtie, that slice of pie is huge."

The older woman chuckled. "I wanted my favorite niece to have a piece large enough she'll never forget what it tastes like."

Carrie grinned up at her. "I've never forgotten how good your pies are, Aunt Myrtie. Thank you."

Her aunt gave her a smile filled with love and started to turn away. "You finish that and then I'll give you a tour of the kitchen so you can meet my new cook. Charlie is a gem. He runs the place in the late afternoons and again for the evening crowd. That way I only have to work until 2 o'clock. God was good when He sent Charlie my way. I don't know what I'd do without him."

She watched her aunt walk away and turned her attention back to the warm piece of pie in front of her with vanilla ice cream melting down the sides. Picking up her fork, she took a bite of the dessert, almost moaning out loud as the tart yet sweet flavors hit her tongue.

Oh, Aunt Myrtie. If you keep feeding me like this, I'll be as big as a whale before I go home.

Forty minutes later, Carrie had officially met Charlie, a young man about Carrie's age, who Myrtle proudly announced had attended culinary school in Nashville. She was also officially introduced to Sadie and Kathy, the two college-aged girls who were working for Aunt Myrtie for the summer, waiting and bussing tables. They were both nineteen and full of dreams for their futures. Carrie looked at them in wonderment. Had she ever been that naïve about the real world? Maybe...once upon a time—before a crazed man had attacked her in her own bedroom.

Since that moment in time, life for her had never been the same.

Carrie tried to clear her head of such thoughts and brought her attention back to her aunt, who was handing out last minute instructions to the crew for the evening menu. She was once again amazed at the abilities of this woman and couldn't help but wonder when Aunt Myrtie was going to retire—or at least slow down a little bit.

"Well, I think that about wraps it up," her aunt said as she untied her apron and threw it in a bin with dirty towels and aprons.

She gave Carrie a beaming smile. "Let's head home."

The Healing Hills

CHAPTER 2

That evening Neil Johnston stopped at *Meyers Place* for an early dinner. He'd closed his gallery a little earlier than normal as it had been a slow day businesswise—and since he'd missed lunch, he'd decided he deserved a tasty hot meal followed by a piece of Miss Myrtie's delicious homemade apple pie. He might even order it al-a mode.

It was still too early for the normal dinner crowd so there wasn't a big crowd in the café, but that was fine with him. Sometimes the noise of a lot of people bothered him, and tonight he just needed a quiet place to enjoy his meal.

A young waitress wearing the nametag of 'Sadie' brought him the meatloaf special with a heaping mound of fluffy mashed potatoes and red-eye gravy with green beans on the side, and filled his coffee cup back to the brim. After she left his table, he dropped his head and closed his eyes for a moment to say thanks for the delicious food before him. God had been so good to him, it seemed only right he thank Him whenever he got the opportunity.

Because of his booth's proximity to the front counter, while Neil ate his meal he couldn't help but overhear the two waitresses discussing Myrtle's recently arrived visitor. It sounded like some family member—maybe a niece—had been at the café earlier in the day and was staying out at the farm with Myrtle. He was glad to hear it. As far as he was concerned, Myrtle Meyers had been alone far too long and he worried about her. She'd taken him under her wings when he'd moved here three years ago, and over time they'd become good friends. He tried to check on her every few days, but after all, he wasn't family. Somewhere in Nashville she had a couple of sons whom she rarely saw by the sounds of things. It just didn't seem right to Neil to have family and ignore them. He'd never met Miss Myrtle's sons, but just the fact that they more or less ignored their elderly mother annoyed him greatly. If he'd had a family somewhere, he would have spent as much time with them as possible. Family was a gift—and not to be taken for granted. He'd learned that the hard way.

The two waitresses were still discussing the niece. "She's kinda cute, don't you think?" "Yeah, I do—although she looked kind of sad too, you know?" "Wonder why she's here? Do you think Miss Myrtie's okay. Sure hope she isn't sick or something."

Neil took a deep breath and tried to turn his attention back to his meal, not wanting to listen to the young gals' gossip—although a part of him found it interesting that these two young gals thought Myrtie's niece was cute. Hopefully he'd have a chance to meet her while she was visiting.

He finished up the last bite of his pie and ice cream, drank the final sip of his coffee, tucked some money under the coffee cup for a tip, and walked over to the counter to pay his bill. The waitress named Kathy quit talking long enough to count back his change, while Sadie grabbed a brown plastic tub and headed over to clean off his table for the next customer.

After exiting *Meyers Place*, Neil stood on the front porch of the building for a moment and took a deep breath, then exhaled before heading to his car. There was nothing quite like fresh mountain air. Plus it was a perfect evening, with just a slight breeze and a clear cloudless sky above him. Running his hand through his curly brown hair, he made the spur of the moment decision to drive into the mountains to see if he could get a few photos before sunset. He should still have several hours of good sun.

In addition to his paintings, Neil also sold framed photographs of the area—candid shots of buildings, people, flowers, and nature. He'd been told he had a good eye for catching the light in such a way that the focal point of his photos almost glowed. He didn't know about that; he just looked through the lens and took the shots that spoke to his heart. But he'd been able to sell quite a few of his photographs over the years to national magazines, along with consistent sales out of his gallery, so it helped pay the bills. His original oils and watercolors also sold well. Neil had been blessed to have a large gallery in Chicago even show some of his work and he'd made several good sales through them over the past few years. Recently, he'd been trying his hand at sculpting and had even sold several of those pieces. His business didn't provide him with the huge salary he'd pulled in when he worked as a Civil Law attorney, but he was his own man here and didn't have to answer to anyone else. His schedule was his own and he truly felt God had blessed him.

Neil had learned four years ago that there were some things much more important than money.

He drove out Highway 73 until he came to the Foothills Parkway, driving several miles until he came to a familiar turnoff, then pulled over, parked, and grabbed his camera out of the back seat. The turnoff was one of his favorite spots in this area. From this lookout you could see mountain ranges for miles—everything from Clingmans Dome to Gregory Bald. The way the light swept over the mountains never failed to amaze him, and he quickly took several shots before the sunlight changed on him. This late in the day there wasn't much traffic on the road behind him, so he wandered around the area with his camera taking additional shots of several kinds of wildflowers and ferns, always on the lookout for something new to photograph.

Eventually the light began to fade and he reluctantly decided it was time to head home. Placing his camera on the seat beside him, Neil began the drive back down the mountain, going slowly with the car windows rolled down. This time just before dark had always been one of his favorites, with the crickets chirping and the peepers peeping, and an occasional night bird or bat swooping through the sky. He kept his eyes peeled on the road in front of him though as you never knew when some four legged critter might step out in front of the car. He'd seen everything from bears and deer to foxes, coyotes and turkeys up in these mountains.

Turning back onto Highway 73, he headed toward his house. Home was a log house he'd built on the lower side of a mountain at the edge of town near the Little River. Neil didn't have much in the way of possessions, but had built the house when he'd first moved here in the hopes it would someday be filled with a family. With three bedrooms, two bathrooms, huge living room and kitchen, and an attached art studio, it was much larger than he needed as a single man. He didn't spent a lot of time at the house though as he tried to spend as much time as he could either in the art studio or at his store/gallery, working. The house was mostly just a place to sleep and occasionally hang out on rainy Sunday afternoons.

It wasn't a real home to him—that was for certain. He hadn't had a real home for a long time– ever since the terrible car accident that had taken his family from him four years earlier.

∧∧∧∧∧

Home.

Carrie felt a wistful smile sweep across her face as she drove out of the parking lot of the restaurant and followed Aunt Myrtie driving her old pickup truck. Ever since her parents had sold the house she'd grown up in just outside of Knoxville and moved to Charlotte, North Carolina, she hadn't felt like she'd had a real home. The apartment she shared with Ashlynn in Lexington certainly wasn't a real home, especially since the attack. Even though they had moved from their original two bedroom apartment into a different one located in a separate building in the same complex, it still gave Carrie the creeps every night to come home from work knowing what had happened there. It would never feel like home to her again. Home should be someplace that made you feel loved and safe; both feelings she had lost since the attack.

Carrie shook her head to eliminate negative thoughts and instead tried to concentrate on keeping track of her aunt's vehicle up ahead. She had been to Aunt Myrtle's farm many times in the past, but after fifteen years, she wasn't sure she'd remember how to get there on her own.

The afternoon sun shone down through the trees as she followed the battered pickup truck around the sides of the mountains, along narrow paved roads, and up and down the rolling hills. She noticed streams of water coming from the craggy rock sides of the hillsides next to the roads, then remembered the earlier rains of the week. Carrie was aware that because it had rained up on top of the mountains, gravity alone required that same rain water come down the mountains somewhere. It was spring, and she was aware from past experiences that water would be gushing down the hillsides everywhere to fill the Little River, Little Pigeon, and all the small creeks and rivers in the area.

Fifteen minutes later they made another sharp turn on the narrow dirt road and the familiar farm and farmhouse of her childhood came into view. Tucked between mountain ranges was the flat valley Myrtle and Jasper Meyers had farmed and lived on ever since they'd married. Now that Jasper was gone, it was just Aunt Myrtie trying to keep the old place up, and Carrie was sure things weren't going to look the same. Uncle Jasper had been a stickler on keeping things just so and she'd spent many a summer helping him paint farm buildings and fences. He had taken great pride in owning a piece of 'God's great world', as he'd often called it and had taken care of each and every foot of his property. Carrie knew from what her aunt had told her that a neighbor was renting the land and doing the farming now, so some of the farmland had been planted into wheat and corn. But it felt strange to Carrie when she realized the land was no longer being farmed by her uncle.

The small two-story farmhouse sat back from the road down a dusty drive, tucked between a grove of majestic pines and sweet gum trees. Back of the house sat the old barn, its flaking red siding looking like it hadn't seen a paint brush in years. There was also a small grove of apple and pear trees, and Carrie was sure her aunt would have a small vegetable garden nearby too. Carrie had spent her share of time during her summers, picking beans and peas and other vegetables from that garden for her Aunt Myrtie to freeze and put up into cans for the winter.

Following Aunt Myrtie's truck, Carrie pulled her car around back of the house and parked next to it. Her aunt had already exited her truck and was carrying what looked like a sack of groceries up the back porch steps. She turned and called down from the porch.

"Come on in, sweetie. As you can see, nothing much has changed around here."

Carrie grabbed her purse from the front seat and got out of the car, and was instantly greeted by a chocolate colored Labrador. This wasn't the dog of her childhood, but it was the same breed. Carrie stopped and let the dog sniff her closed hand, and before she knew it she was being welcomed with a swishing tail and a friendly lick.

"That's Buster," Aunt Myrtie announced. "After old Willy got hit by a car seven years ago, I went to the Humane Society and found this dog. He was just a pup and was so doggone cute, I just fell in love with him. He's been a good guard dog and keeps me company. But neither of us gets around as quickly as we used to."

Carrie quickly followed her aunt up the back porch steps, through the back door, and into the familiar farmhouse kitchen. It was a large room with white painted wooden cupboards topped by dark gray Formica countertops running the length of the outside wall. Lacy white curtains hung at a large multi-paned window overlooking the back yard. A well-used round oak table and chairs sat in the middle of the room, with a refrigerator and stove on the opposite wall. Carrie knew from past experience, there was no built-in dishwasher or microwave in this kitchen.

She also knew every part of this house had been lovingly built by Myrtle's husband, Uncle Jasper, and her own Great-Grandpa Clyde Foust—Myrtle's father. After Aunt Myrtie and Uncle Jasper married, they had built the house large enough so Great-Grandpa and Great-Grandma Foust could live with them. After Great-Grandma passed away though, Clyde Foust had preferred living by himself in the cabin up on the side of the mountain—until he had become so feeble he had been forced to move back into the old farmhouse with them until his death.

This old house held so many wonderful memories for Carrie. She knew that through the open doorway sat a small dining room, and through there was the 'front room', as it was called—filled with several overstuffed chairs, small tables, and a couch. At one end of that room sat a huge stone fireplace with a beautifully carved wooden mantle and low bookshelves on both sides. Off the front room was a small bedroom and bathroom which was always Aunt Myrtle's & Uncle Jasper's. She was sure her aunt was still using it. Carrie also knew that upstairs were two more bedrooms and a bathroom—the beds covered with colorful patchwork quilts, and lacy curtains hanging at the windows. And everything would be spotless, just like the kitchen she was standing in. That's how Aunt Myrtie did things.

She watched her aunt place the sack of groceries on the counter, along with her purse and keys. As she stared at the room around her, Carrie couldn't believe the memories that rushed through her at being here again; although there was one thing that was glaring in its omission. There was no Uncle Jasper to come and give her one of his ginormous hugs, or pick her up and swing her through the air like a pendulum, calling her 'his little gal'. Carrie swallowed hard at the memories that threatened to choke her up. She could only imagine how much Aunt Myrtie missed him.

Carrie watched Aunt Myrtie pull two Styrofoam boxes out of the bottom of the sack, and then reach in the kitchen drawer to pull out silverware.

"I didn't get any lunch. I know you did, Carrie, but if you're still hungry and want to join me...." Aunt Myrtie pointed in the direction of the table and chairs.

Grabbing one of the boxes of food from her aunt, Carrie went over and took a seat at the well-worn table. She opened the lid enough to peek in and was rewarded with the aroma of garlic and tomatoes.

"Lasagna," she almost whispered. "Oh Aunt Myrtie, I haven't had your lasagna in years."

Aunt Myrtie laughed, then grabbed Carrie's free hand to say grace. "Thank you, dear Lord, for this food we're about to eat. Thank you for the beautiful day you have given us. And a special thank you for finally bringing my prodigal niece back home. I've missed her so much. Please bless her and give her peace, and let her know without a doubt how much she is loved."

Carrie squeezed her aunt's hand and blinked as tears formed in the corner of her eyes at the words of the prayer. Aunt Myrtie couldn't have any idea of how important it was for her to have peace again. Ever since the attack, she had known nothing but fear and apprehension, and self-loathing…like it had somehow been her fault that she'd been attacked. The psychiatrist told her that was a normal reaction, but that there was no way she was responsible for what the crazed man had done to her. Carrie still couldn't erase the feeling of somehow being to blame from her psyche though.

With Aunt Myrtie's final amen, Carrie took a deep breath to clear her thoughts, and picked up her fork to delve into the lasagna. As she took the first bite, she almost groaned in appreciation as the flavors hit her taste buds. How could she still be hungry? It hadn't been that long since she'd eaten her lunch.

"Oh, this is so good," she finally mumbled around her bites of food. "I can't believe I'm eating this after chowing down all that lunch you fed me, but this is soooo good."

Aunt Myrtie chuckled. "I'm glad you enjoy it. I know, I know—I make food all day for people, but there's something special about cookin' for family."

Carrie reached across the table and touched her aunt's arm. "I'm sorry I haven't been back sooner. It's not that I didn't want to come back, it's just…."

"I understand," the other woman interrupted, waving her fork through the air. "Life got in the way. I hear the same thing from my boys. If I'm lucky, I get to see them and the grandkids once or twice a year around my birthday or at Thanksgiving and Christmas." She gave Carrie a gentle smile. "I've just missed you, that's all."

"Well," Aunt Myrtie continued. "You're here now, and we're going to make the best of the time you're here. I, for one, am going to enjoy every minute of it." She stood and took her dirty silverware and now empty food container over to the kitchen sink.

"If you want, once you finish eating, we can go up to the cabin." She turned and glanced back at Carrie. "Are you sure you want to stay up there by yourself though? I have plenty of space here and you know you're more than welcome to stay with me if you'd rather not be alone right now."

Carrie finished chewing her last bite of lasagna. "Thanks, Aunt Myrtie. But I'm sure. I think it will do me good." She smiled. "I brought along plenty of books and my laptop with me. Plus I want to work on collecting history about our family, so I'll spend a lot of time doing that. And I plan to be gone from the cabin during the day most of the time anyway—seeing the sights again. I'll be fine."

Her aunt nodded. "Okay, but remember, if the solitude gets to be too much for you, my offer still stands." She gave Carrie a little grin. "And if you get really bored, you're more than welcome to come to *Meyers Place* any time you want."

Carrie heard her aunt's chuckle and couldn't help but smile in return. She was reminded of summers past when she'd complain about being bored. It didn't take long before either Uncle Jasper or Aunt Myrtie would come up with a task that needed to be done, and Carrie's time of boredom was soon over. There wasn't time for relaxing on a farm—or in a restaurant, she was sure.

They finished cleaning up the kitchen and headed out the door, this time both of them getting in Carrie's car. Carrie recalled how steep the drive was up to the cabin. There was no way Aunt Myrtle would be able to walk back down the mountainside by herself, so she knew she'd have to bring her back down to her house later. Right now though, it felt good knowing she wouldn't be entering the cabin for the first time by herself. She closed her eyes for a second and literally stiffened her back as she turned the key to start her car's ignition. If she planned to stay there alone for the summer, she was going to have to get used to the solitude—especially during the evenings.

The gravel lane that led up to the cabin hadn't changed much over the years, although it seemed to Carrie that the brush and trees were growing inward toward the lane even more, making it narrower than ever. As they slowly made their way up the mountainside, the tires on her car spit out stones and dust as she sharply turned the wheel to take the next curve. Aunt Myrtie chattered all the way, seemingly unaffected by the steep drive. She explained to Carrie where things were in the cabin and told her the best places in town to buy her groceries and meat. Carrie attempted to listen while still concentrating on staying on the road. In a few minutes they'd traversed the steep trail and came out to a flatter area which opened to a small yard. Sitting in the middle of the clearing was the old cabin her great-grandfather, Clyde Foust, had built when he and his wife, Cora Beth, had first moved here. They'd had to leave their farm in Cades Cove, a nearby valley which had been the home of many families, when the land had been purchased by the government for inclusion into the Great Smoky National Park.

Carrie pulled her car around to the side of the cabin and parked it, and took a moment to make sure all the windows were rolled up tight. It wouldn't do for some critter like a squirrel or raccoon—or even a bear—to get in the car overnight.

Aunt Myrtie was out of the car and up on the porch before Carrie could even haul one of her suitcases out of the trunk. She lugged the heavy case up the wooden steps onto the porch and followed her aunt through the cabin's heavy wooden door.

"I've been up here and cleaned recently, 'cause I knew you were coming, so I don't think it should be very dirty. Although you might want to open the windows so the place has a chance to air out a little bit. I don't remember when somebody last stayed here for more than a night or two. It's been years."

Carrie dropped her bags near the door and looked around the old cabin. It was just as she remembered. The front part of the cabin was one large room, with a living room and huge stone fireplace at one end, and a small kitchen at the other end. She knew the side door went out to a small porch, and an area where there used to be a small herb garden. In the rear part of the cabin was a good-sized bedroom and a bathroom.

The cabin was old, but had been completely modernized back in the early 1960s with insulation, plumbing, and electricity in the walls, which were then dry walled. Inside the cabin the only bare log walls still showing were the ones between the living area and the bedroom and bathroom. But the flooring was still the original wide pine boards and were waxed and polished to a glow. Faded oval braided rugs graced the areas in front of the comfortable looking dark brown sofa and oak coffee table, and there was another rug covering the wooden floor next to the bed in the bedroom. Wandering through the door to the bathroom, Carrie took inventory of the fluffy towels and washcloths on the shelves.

Aunt Myrtie might not have thought the place was clean enough, but to Carrie, it looked spotless.

She walked back out into the main room where her aunt waited for her. "Everything looks great, Aunt Myrtie. I can't tell you how much I appreciate you letting me stay here."

The older woman pulled her into an unexpected hug, and once again Carrie caught the whiff of onions and celery she knew came from her aunt working in the diner.

"What do you mean 'let you stay here'? You're family, girl, and this cabin is meant for family to use. My Daddy would love the thought that his great-granddaughter is spending her summer here." She chuckled. "And you just remember, if you get too bored, you can always come to the restaurant and I'll find something for you to do."

Carrie laughed as her aunt released her from her embrace. It had been so long since she'd had the adult hugs of her childhood; it felt kind of good to be treated like a child again, even if just for a moment.

"I will, Aunt Myrtie. And you remember, if you need me for anything, just give me a call on my cell phone."

Her aunt spent a few more minutes explaining where everything was in the kitchen, which she had even stocked with a few groceries.

"I didn't want you to arrive and have no food to start out with, so I went and picked up a few items I thought might need, like milk, eggs, bread, etc. I figured tomorrow you can fill up the larder the way you want, but this should get you through tonight and tomorrow morning."

She also reminded Carrie how to use the fireplace, explaining about opening the damper and how to get the kindling started. Carrie listened carefully while the older woman described the steps to her. It had been a long time since she'd started a fire, and the last thing Carrie wanted to do was burn down her family's ancestral cabin.

"There's a big stack of wood out back in the small shed," Aunt Myrtle added. "Although I don't imagine you'll want to burn too many fires once the weather warms up."

Carrie looked around the cabin a little more with Aunt Myrtle tagging along behind her, reminiscing about how it had been when her mother and father were living there. Then it was time to take her aunt back down the mountainside to her house, and make the return drive back up to the cabin.

Alone.

Once she returned to the cabin, Carrie sat outside on the front porch in one of the wooden rocking chairs and enjoyed the view of the countryside around her. From this viewpoint on the side of the mountain, she could see through the trees and down the hill to her aunt's farm, then across the valley to the mountains on the other side. The layers and layers of hills in the distance seemed to go on forever. Carrie noticed there was now a little green in the color of the mountains which meant the buds on the trees were finally starting to pop open. It wouldn't be long and those same hillsides would be rich with the colors of different shades of green, then the brilliant hues of dogwood, mountain laurel, and rhododendron blossoms would spread over the area.

Carrie sighed in contentment while she slowly rocked the chair and soaked up the view. She heard a couple of mourning doves call out to each other in the woods next to the cabin. Other than that, there was silence.

She smiled a little smile and allowed her head to rest against the back of the rocker. This was why she had left the city. There was a peace here she couldn't get anywhere else. When her mom had originally suggested coming here, she had hesitated at first. Then the happy memories of her childhood had urged her to return to the place of her ancestors. Maybe here she could recover the person she had been before the attack.

Looking out at the mountains, she couldn't help but remember a Bible verse from her past church-going days.

I will lift up mine eyes unto the hills, from whence cometh my help.

She didn't know the exact place it could be found in the Bible other than she thought it was in the book of Psalm. But it didn't matter where it was; it seemed rather fitting for this moment in her life, with the hills surrounding her like a cocoon.

She truly hoped and prayed the verse was accurate and this could be a healing time for her.

∧∧∧∧

A little while later, after the skies in the west were streaked with the dark yellows, oranges, and reds of a beautiful sunset, the peepers and crickets started chirping louder, and the evening mists moved in through the trees—along with the bugs. Carrie finally decided it was time to go inside and get ready for bed—making sure to first secure the deadbolt on the front door and side door of the cabin. She had to admit, for all her brave words to her aunt, she was a little apprehensive about being alone up here at night. Daytime solitude didn't bother her, but when the darkness of the night moved in, the demons of what had happened haunted her. She was a big girl though; surely she could do this. Besides, one of the great things about being up here on the side of the mountain—no one could drive up that steep dirt road without her hearing them coming.

Glancing around the cabin one more time to see that everything was as it should be, she turned out the lights in the living room and went into the bedroom, scuffing her bare feet out of her slippers as she reached the bed. There was only a moment's pause before she turned off the lamp on the bedside stand and climbed under the covers. While she listened to the stillness of the night around her, she sighed and tried to get comfortable in the unfamiliar bed. She had forgotten how quiet it was in the country—well, other than the sound of the night peepers and crickets drifting through the bedroom window she'd left cracked open a few inches. Carrie turned over on her side and pulled the covers up to her shoulders and sighed again as she closed her eyes. In only a matter of minutes she had turned onto to her back again and was staring into the darkness as a remembered fear swept over her. Instantly she was engulfed in a familiar terror that caused her body to break into a cold sweat.

Had she heard footsteps on the front porch, or was that rustle of leaves outside her window caused by someone walking outside the cabin?

Her mind instantly returned to the night when she'd been attacked. She could almost feel the tip of the knife on her throat and smell his sweat as he held her down. Her body trembled as the awful memories of that night took over and she sobbed as she curled into the fetal position. She had just pulled the covers up over her head in terror when sanity finally kicked in.

There was no one else in the cabin. Nobody was outside her window. It was just her imagination playing tricks on her—again—in the form of another flashback. She'd had plenty of those in the months since the attack and had come to recognize them for what they were. She hated the tricks her mind played on her when the fear took over. She shook her head in disgust at herself. When was she going to get over it and be normal again?

Nights had been like this for her ever since the attack. Her fear had been so intense back in the city, she had started leaving a light on in her bedroom. Fortunately, Ashlynn was such a good friend she hadn't given her a rough time about it—knowing what she had been through. But Carrie had hoped that here, in the country, she wouldn't feel this awful suffocating fear anymore. She hadn't had this bad an episode in months.

Maybe coming here where she'd be all alone hadn't been a good idea after all.

Carrie finally gave up and sat on the edge of the bed, turned the lamp back on, then got out of bed and padded through the cabin to double-check the deadbolts on both the front and side doors. Satisfied to find the locks secure, she walked back to the bedroom, then paused in front of the closet and turned the light on, leaving the door partially open to allow some light to filter into the room. Heading back to the bed, she turned off the lamp, finding some level of comfort in the soft light glowing from the closet doorway.

Hot tears pricked her eyes as she squeezed her eyelids shut and turned over in bed again. Would she ever feel safe again?

The Healing Hills

CHAPTER 3

Carrie woke up the next morning to bright sunlight streaming into the bedroom through the sheer curtains, and the cheerful sounds of birds' songs coming through the open window. After a tough time getting to sleep the night before, she had finally dozed off about midnight and slept straight through the night. Thankfully, once she finally fell asleep, her slumber had been relatively nightmare free. She hadn't had many nights like that since the attack.

She stretched out in bed, then threw the covers off and plodded barefoot to the kitchen to start a pot of coffee in the coffeemaker before she headed to the bathroom for a shower. Twenty minutes later she had eaten some two pieces of toast slathered with some of Aunt Myrtle's homemade strawberry jam and was sitting in the rocking chair on the front porch. While she sipped her second mug of steaming coffee, she listened to the sounds around her of the mountains waking up. White fluffy clouds drifted across the blue sky with a few low lying clouds lightly touching the tops of the most distant mountains. A misty blue haze rested across the now greening hills.

It was easy to see where the name 'Smoky Mountains' had come from. Her Uncle Jasper had once told her the place was named by the Cherokees hundreds of years earlier. They had called this area *Shaconage*–'Place of Blue Smoke'– The Smokies; and as far as Carrie was concerned, there wasn't another place like it anywhere in the world.

Various birds in the trees above and around her sang their morning songs and she sat and sipped her coffee and listened for a while before deciding it was time for her to start her day. She had no set schedule, but there were certain things she wanted to get accomplished. First, she needed to go to town and buy more groceries. Aunt Myrtie had been kind enough to put a few things in her kitchen, but they were only the basics. She couldn't live on bread and jam and coffee the rest of the summer.

Next, she needed to go to the library and use their free Wi-Fi to check her email and follow up with Ashlynn to make sure she remembered to forward Carrie's mail to her every few days. She also needed to contact Dr. Susan Martin, the Christian therapist recommended to her by her therapist back in Lexington, and make an appointment. Carrie was supposed to continue her sessions here in Tennessee; that was part of the deal with her school.

Then . . . Carrie frowned as she grabbed her purse, keys, and laptop bag. Then she wasn't sure what she was going to do with herself. Maybe she'd just drive around the area and see what she could see. It had been a lot of years since she'd visited. Perhaps playing the role of tourist wouldn't be all that bad.

Carrie slowly drove her car down the steep and curvy narrow dirt lane that led her to the rear property of Aunt Myrtie's farm. Her aunt's pickup was already gone from its normal parking spot when she drove by the house, but that didn't surprise Carrie. She knew her aunt would have been up before daylight in order to get to *Meyers Place* and prepare things to open at six a.m. Carrie felt a moment or two of guilt as she remembered that at that time, she had been in her bed, fast asleep. Then she remembered this was supposed to be a vacation of sorts. Maybe after a few days of rest and relaxation she would stop in the restaurant to see if there was anything she could do to help out; but not yet. She'd only just arrived.

She drove the few miles to the main road which took her back into town. When she drove by her aunt's restaurant, she wasn't surprised to see the parking lot almost full. It was breakfast-time—plus she knew there were a great many townspeople who would just hang out there and drink coffee for an hour or two and catch up on all the latest gossip. It had been that way when she'd visited as a child, and she was sure it hadn't changed any in the last fifteen years.

Driving through town she noted the location of the new grocery store. She would have to stop there and stock up before she headed back to the cabin. The downtown area of the small town looked well-kept, and even had a few shops in the older brick buildings. There were also a couple of more modern looking gas stations, and two churches. A newer frame building with a white sign out front declared it to be the library, so she quickly flipped on her turn signal and turned into their parking area. She grabbed her laptop bag from the seat next to her and headed through their front door, amazed at how large the building was. It didn't look that big from the outside, but inside, rows and rows of waist-high or higher bookshelves spread out in front of her with a large counter at one side.

An older woman glanced up from her stool behind the counter and gave Carrie a friendly smile. Carrie immediately headed toward her.

"Good morning," Carrie said quietly, not wanting to disturb the other patrons sitting around at tables. "I'm interested in using your free Wi-Fi. Is there anything I need to know to access it?"

The older woman smiled and shook her head. "Nope. It's wide open access. You can set up anywhere here in the library." She chuckled with a mischievous grin on her face.

"You could probably sit out in your car and access it if you really wanted to. But it's much more comfortable in here," she smiled and added in a whisper.

Carrie grinned back at her. "Thank you."

She walked through the large area near the front and took a seat at one of the big wooden tables, then pulled her laptop out of the bag and booted up her machine. It wasn't long and she was able to check her email. Ashlynn had sent her an email the day before, assuring her she would forward all her mail like she had asked. She also said she'd checked with the school administration and they'd told her Carrie's last paycheck for the year would be electronically deposited into her checking account as normal, at the end of the month. Carrie quickly typed out an email in response, letting Ashlynn knew she had arrived without any trouble and was trying to relax and enjoy herself. After checking a few more things online, Carrie logged off, put her laptop back in the bag, and waved at the woman behind the counter as she left the library.

One thing on her to-do list was accomplished.

After leaving the library, Carrie decided to do a little sightseeing around town and check out some of the stores. She remembered Aunt Myrtle's mentioning the man who had painted the pictures in the restaurant and that he had a store somewhere here in town. Maybe there were other local artisans with shops too.

It didn't take her long to find the row of stores—called the *Mountain Laurel Mall*. A cluster of newer frame buildings with cedar siding and green metal roofs were grouped together in a small complex with a paved parking lot and sidewalks running between them. There was also a small park-like area out back of the stores with picnic tables under some tall shade trees, and even several swings for the kids. It looked like a pleasant area to do some shopping, and had obviously been created to make families feel comfortable there.

Before she got out of her car, she gazed through her windshield at each building. It looked like there was a quilt shop with colorful patchwork quilts clearly visible through the shop's front window. Another shop had wood carvings and several rustic looking picture frames in the window display. One store was called *The Beekeeper*, so Carrie had to assume they sold locally raised honey—and jams and jellies too by the looks of their front window displays. There was also a pottery store, a store that looked like it specialized in knit and crotched items, and at the very end of a row of buildings, sat the shop she was looking for—*Johnston Photography and Paintings*. Instead of cedar wood siding, this building was a log structure with a little covered porch on the front. It did have the green metal roof though so it carried on the same design as the rest of the buildings while still standing out from the crowd.

Carrie grabbed her purse and got out of her car. It looked like several of the shops weren't open yet, and those that were didn't have many customers. Tourist season wouldn't really start until the schools up north were out for the summer, so it wasn't surprising. As far as she was concerned though, the less busy it was, the better for her since she'd be able to stroll through the stores without having to fight the summer crowds.

The closest store was the quilt shop, so she decided to start there. She pulled open the glass door and then smiled as she heard the sound of a little bell jingle above her. Hearing that sound reminded her of her childhood when she and her Uncle Jasper would go to the local hardware store. They'd had a bell hanging above their door too which rang whenever the door was opened. As she looked around this store, she tried to keep from staring. This certainly wasn't a hardware store. Colorful, full-sized quilts and wall hangings were everywhere, along with shelves covered with quilting magazines, bolts of beautiful calico print material, and spools of multi-colored thread. Her mom, who was an avid sewer, would love this store.

A woman who looked to be in her mid-forties stepped around a wooden counter to greet her.

"Good morning. May I help you find something?"

Carrie smiled at the woman and shook her head. "I'm just looking to see what you have. I'm sorry to say, I'm not a quilter. My mom is though." Carrie continued to gaze around the store in awe. "She really needs to see this place."

The woman, who introduced herself as Willa Marsten, chatted about all the items she carried in her store, and asked Carrie more about what her interests were. When Carrie left the store, she was signed up to receive a monthly email newsletter with updates about the store's products. Not that she'd ever use them, but she supposed she could forward the emails to her mom.

After leaving the quilt shop, Carrie stopped to peer in the windows of a couple of other stores that weren't open yet, taking note of their hours on the signs. It looked like the pottery shop and the woodcarving shop weren't open for business today, but the store that sold jams and jellies was. When she walked through the front door of that shop, she felt like a little kid in a candy store. She wandered down the aisles and surveyed the shelves loaded with colorful jars of honey, jams, jellies, and marmalades. There was also a wide array of cheeses, and some canned specialty items such as chow-chow, relishes, salsas, and pickled eggs. By the time she'd met the owner and chatted a bit, strolled through the store, and purchased a large selection of jars of jams and honey, her mouth was watering. After leaving the store, which was called *Sweet Jams*, she strolled down the sidewalk with her bag of yummy purchases banging against her leg.

She stopped in front of the next shop—*The Johnston Photography and Paintings Gallery*—and tugged the door open. Aunt Myrtie had been insistent that Carrie check out Mr. Johnston's paintings further, but she didn't know why she was bothering. It wasn't like she was going to buy anything. The few framed paintings hanging on the wall of the restaurant were good, but she didn't have any place in her apartment for displaying anything like them. First of all, it wasn't the type of artwork Ashlynn would want hanging on their walls back home anyway. Ashlynn preferred more modern furnishings and abstract art. Besides, Carrie was sure all the paintings would be out of her price range.

Walking through the doorway, she was pleasantly surprised at how bright and airy the open showroom was. Ample sunlight streamed through a wall of tall windows, and as she raised her eyes to the ceiling, she noted this building's ceiling had not been dropped but instead was open all the way to the rafters. Large skylights in the roof allowed even more light to come into the shop.

She dropped her eyes from the ceiling to scan the inside of the store. Framed photographs and paintings hung on every available wall, with several shorter walls set up in the middle of the large room, creating aisles. Shelving along the outside walls held smaller framed photographs of wild turkeys, bears, birds, and wildflowers, and even several small sculptures.

Carrie wandered across the showroom floor toward one huge framed oil painting hanging on the wall that immediately caught her eye. It was a painting of the Carter Shields cabin in Cades Cove in the springtime, with leaves bursting out on the trees, and the dogwoods showing off their blossoms. She stopped in front of the oil painting and gazed at how the light filtered down through the trees—just the way she remembered from the last time she had been to that particular spot. She could almost envision herself walking down the familiar pathway to the cabin, the sound of the last year's leaves crunching under her feet, hearing the song birds in the trees around her, and the squeaking and scurrying of chipmunks as they darted off the path and into the woods.

The painting was good—really good.

∧∧∧∧∧

Neil Johnston watched from behind the counter as the young woman came through the door of his store, pause for a moment, and then look around her as if in awe. It was a common reaction from his customers the first time they entered the store, and he loved it. From the outside most people wouldn't think the structure would look like this on the inside, and he had spent a great deal of time designing it in such a way that it would be airy and filled with light—the better to show off his art.

After her perusal of the raised ceiling, the young woman's eyes seemed to immediately focus on his large oil of the Carter Shields cabin which hung on the wall directly in line with the front door. He watched as she headed straight toward it. She didn't look like a local, nor was she anyone he could recall being in his shop before, and he was sure he would have remembered her. With her slim build and gorgeous straight blond hair—the color of golden flax—hanging just past her shoulders, she was very attractive.

He stepped out from behind the counter and headed her way.

"Have you ever been to Cades Cove to see the Carter Shields cabin in person?" he asked as he came up behind her. He must have startled her as she gave a nervous jerk, then turned around to look at him with a look of panic on her face.

He quickly apologized. "I'm sorry. I didn't mean to sneak up behind you like that."

She gave what sounded like a nervous laugh and quickly replaced the look of fear he'd seen with a little smile. "Oh, that's okay. I was just lost in the painting for a moment and didn't hear you."

She turned back to look at the painting again and gave a little nod. "Yes, I've been to the Cove—many times during my childhood. It's been a few years though."

"You're from around here then?"

The young woman shook her head and Neil was mesmerized by the way the light coming through the skylights in the ceiling played across her hair. The painter in him wondered if it would ever be possible to catch that color and light in a portrait—and her skin was flawlessly clear.

"No, just visiting family for the summer."

Neil caught his breath as she turned her face to his and he saw beautiful blue eyes staring back at him. They were eyes you could stare into forever and lose track of what you were going to say—which he did.

"I love this painting," she finally turned back to the framed oil hanging on the wall and the spell was broken. "It truly catches the beauty of that particular spot in the Cove."

"Thanks," he mumbled, then cleared his throat. "It's one of my favorites too."

She chuckled as she pointed at the price tag and then looked up at him again. "I'm afraid it's a little out of my price range though."

He grinned at her. He didn't take any offense at her remark as he knew not everyone could afford his original paintings. Most of his higher priced oils sold to collectors from the city, or to interior decorators working on a commission to furnish properties in the more urban areas. Every now and then he sold one of the nicer ones to one of the many tourists that wandered in off the sidewalk, but those occasions were rare.

"I have framed reproductions over here, if you're interested." He led her across the room to where smaller copies of the larger oil paintings hung on a wall. Neil watched as she surveyed the framed copies until she found the one she was looking for.

"This is more in my budget range. Thank you."

They walked together toward the opposite side of the showroom where the counter and cash register sat.

"Can I interest you in anything else, Miss . . ." Neil specifically left the opening, hoping the young woman would take the hint that he was searching for her full name.

"I'm Carrie. And I think this is all I can afford this time. I feel like I just spend half my inheritance at the jam and jelly store." She laughed that musical little laugh of hers and he found himself smiling broadly while he rang up her purchase and wrapped her framed painting.

"Well, Carrie. It was a pleasure to meet you. I'm Neil Johnston and I hope you come back again—even if you don't purchase anything. I enjoyed talking with you."

She gave him a shy little smile as she paid for her purchase, took her package from him, and gave a little wave as she turned and left the gallery.

Neil walked over to the doorway after she left and watched her stroll down the sidewalk and out of his life, then released a huge sigh. She was a beauty, but obviously not interested in him. She had almost seemed frightened of him at first—beyond shy—and had been very hesitant about even telling him her name, but he was glad he had asked her.

Carrie.

It was the perfect name for her. He closed his eyes and pictured again the way the light shone on her hair. He didn't ever want to forget how that looked. Sorry to say though, he would more than likely never see her again. If she was just visiting the area, she would be like all the tourists that came through his door. Here one day and gone the next. And he didn't even know her last name.

He turned back to his work with another sigh of resignation.

As Neil walked back toward the counter where the cash register sat, his eyes fell on the clock hanging on the wall behind the counter. It was almost noon, and the way his stomach was grumbling, it was time to close the store for a bit and find some good food to eat, and he knew exactly where he would go.

∧∧∧∧∧

A few minutes later he was seated at a small table at the *Meyers Place Restaurant*, waiting for his order to arrive. It wasn't too busy in the small diner today, which meant Myrtle Meyers, the owner, had time to visit with him while she poured him a second cup of coffee.

"How ya doin' today, Neil?" she asked.

Neil had grown rather attached to the older woman in the three years he'd been living here. She reminded him of her own grandmother, who had passed away several years ago. He would often run out to the farm to help Myrtle with something—or just to check in on her and make sure she was okay. Not that she'd ever asked for his help; she was one independent woman, but then, he supposed she'd had to be without having her husband to help her out all these years.

"Doing fine, Miss Myrtle. Even made a sale this morning."

He heard Myrtle's chuckle.

"That's a very good thing, young man, especially if you want to keep that gallery of yours open."

Neil winked and gave her a little grin. "Yes, ma'am."

She surprised him by sitting down in the chair across the table from him. "So tell me; what are you doing tonight for dinner, Neil? Would you be interested in some home-cookin'?"

He looked up from his mug of coffee in surprise to find the hazel eyes behind her glasses studying him closely. It had been quite a while since she'd invited him out to the farm for a meal.

"I'd never turn away one of your home-cooked meals, Miss Myrtle. You know that."

A huge smile swept over her face. "Good! Then I'll see you at six o'clock. You can come earlier, if you want." She stood up and picked the pot of coffee back up off the table and readied to leave.

"Got somebody I want you to meet."

With those words, she turned and walked back toward the kitchen, leaving him feeling like he'd been side-swiped. It sounded like he was being set up to meet this niece from the city everyone had been talking about the day before. He wasn't sure if that was a good idea or not, but he'd already accepted the invitation. There was no backing out now without hurting Miss Myrtle's feelings, and he certainly didn't want to do that. Besides, a home cooked meal sounded too good to pass up.

CHAPTER 4

By the time Carrie stopped at the grocery store and filled a cart with all the items she needed, it was way past her lunchtime. She'd originally planned on going to the restaurant to see Aunt Myrtie, but with her favorite chocolate chip ice cream melting in the back seat of her car, she decided that would have to wait for another day. Besides, she was tired after all her running around. Going back to the cabin and resting for a while sounded heavenly.

She drove her car up the steep lane to the parking area next to the cabin and let out a sigh of relief at having made it up without any trouble. It was a good thing they didn't get much snow in this part of Tennessee. That drive would be treacherous during an icy or snowy winter.

It took Carrie three trips to get all her purchases out of the car and into the cabin. When she finally placed the last sack on the table, she let out a sigh of relief. With the amount of groceries she'd purchased, she should be set for a while.

She put the cold and frozen items away, then left the other items in their sacks and instead turned to the package holding the framed painting reproduction she had purchased at Neil Johnston's gallery. As she pulled it out and gazed at it, she was instantly transported back to his shop when she stood in front of the large original oil painting. She wasn't a big fan of art, but she really loved that painting. This one wasn't as impressive in size, but it was still beautiful, and the scene was so quiet and peaceful. It gave her comfort to look at it.

Now. What should she do with it?

Strolling around the cabin with the painting in her hands, she finally stopped in front of the fireplace mantel, moved a couple of small framed photographs around, and placed her new purchase in the center, leaning it up against the stones of the back wall of the fireplace. She took a step or two back, tipped her head to get a couple of different perspectives, and gave a sign of contentment. It was perfect, and now every time she saw it she would be reminded of her most favorite place in the whole world—Cades Cove. Maybe it wouldn't fit in very well with the décor of the rest of the apartment back in the city, but she would just have to keep it in her bedroom on her dresser or something. There was no way she was giving up this one—even for her roommate, Ashlynn.

Once that job was accomplished, Carrie took a few moments to put away the rest of the groceries, and then fixed herself a quick sandwich, taking the plate and a glass of iced tea out on the front porch to eat. With the bright sun beating down, the air had warmed up considerably, and the sky was a perfect cobalt blue. Carrie was no artist, but seeing the cloudless blue sky, her thoughts returned to Neil Johnston and his paintings. Even as talented as he appeared to be, she wondered if he would be able to catch the beauty of this day in oils.

After she ate her lunch, she grabbed her cell phone and made the much avoided call to Dr. Martin, the therapist in Maryville she was supposed to go see. She talked to the receptionist and made an appointment for the next week. She was dreading having to go through the details of the attack with another counselor, but she also knew it was necessary to do it if she ever wanted to go back to work.

Hopefully this Dr. Martin would help her deal with the attack so that the nightmares and fears would go away.

She was tired of living with it.

A little later after cleaning up her lunch dishes, she wandered around the living room of the cabin as a restlessness swept over her. She stopped in front of the small bookshelf in the corner of the living room and lightly ran her fingers across the spines of the books. Most of the books were the old classics—*Little Women, Black Beauty, Around the World in Eighty Days, Robinson Crusoe, Far From the Maddening Crowd*—books she had grown up reading. There was also what looked like a well-worn Bible. Carrie pulled it off the shelf and ran her hand gently across the front of it, and then opened the front cover. Inside was a name written in elaborate cursive; *Clyde Foust*. She let out a little gasp of joy at the realization that she was holding her great-grandfather's Bible.

She carefully flipped through the worn pages until an underlined verse caught her eye. *For God hath not given us the spirit of fear; but of power, and of love, and of a sound mind.* She gently closed the book and held it against her chest. What a perfect verse for her. It was as if her great-grandfather had known someday she would need to read this very verse at a time in her life that was filled with fear. A sense of nostalgia swept over her. She'd never had a chance to know Clyde Foust since he'd passed away when she was a toddler, but she'd heard stories about him during the summers she'd spent here in the mountains.

Clyde had actually been the one who built the very cabin she was standing in, back in the mid-1930s. When he and his wife, Cora Beth, had to leave their home in Cades Cove, Clyde had built this one. When the government had bought up all the land to turn the Cove into part of the Great Smoky Mountains National Park, the Fousts had reluctantly joined the others in their community in selling their land and moving out. Carrie had heard stories over the years about how Cora Beth had died just a few months after they'd left the Cove. The romantic side of her had always felt it must have been from a broken heart at having to leave her home. After his wife's death, Clyde had lived the remainder of his life alone, here in this cabin back of Jasper and Myrtle's farm.

It made Carrie sad to think she had no memories of her great-grandfather. She had been told that he had held her on his lap and rocked her in his rocker on the front porch of this very cabin, telling her stories of how life had been back in the Cove. It made her feel sad that she couldn't remember him.

She carefully placed the old Bible on the table in front of the sofa along with her laptop and several other books she planned on reading. After finding that verse in the Bible about fear, it got her to thinking. Maybe later she would spend some time looking for that verse she had remembered her first night here—the one about lifting her eyes unto the hills. She would really like to read more of the Bible too. She had one back home somewhere, stuck in a drawer or packed away in a box. Perhaps it was time she started reading it again and seeing what the Bible had to say about life. After everything she'd been through in the past year, it sure couldn't hurt, and there had been a time when scripture had meant a lot to her.

About that time, her cell phone rang and she scurried to find it, finally locating it on the kitchen counter with her purse.

"Hello."

"Hi, sweetie. It's Aunt Myrtie."

Carrie smiled at the thought that her Aunt Myrtle felt it necessary to identify herself.

"Hi, yourself, Aunt Myrtie. What's up?" Carrie walked over and plopped down on the sofa.

"Just wondered if you'd like to come down to the house for supper tonight? I'm fixing fried chicken, mashed potatoes, and cherry cobbler."

Carrie laughed out loud at the sound of blatant bribery coming from the other end of the phone. "Aunt Myrtle, you don't have to entice me to come to dinner—although for that food, I wouldn't miss it for the world. What time do you want me there?"

"How about five-thirty? That way you can help set the table and such."

She grinned. "I'll be there—and thanks again for the invite!"

As she disconnected the call, she grinned. At least she wouldn't have to worry about what she was going to fix for dinner tonight.

∧∧∧∧∧

Neil glanced down at his wristwatch and groaned as he locked the front door of his gallery. It had been a busy afternoon and time had gotten away from him. Now he was going to be late for dinner at Myrtle Meyers' house. He thought about calling her to let her know he was going to be tardy, but finally decided he'd just get a nice bouquet of flowers at the flower shop and go.

Hopefully Miss Myrtle wouldn't chew him out too much for not arriving on time.

Fifteen minutes later he was pulling down the familiar dirt drive that took him to her house. He was surprised to see another car already parked next to Miss Myrtle's pickup, but pulled his Jeep in next to that one and hurriedly got out. Myrtle was already waiting at the back door, holding it open with her hip, and a look of concern on her face.

"I was starting to get worried about you, Neil Johnston."

He shook his head in dismay. He knew he should have called. "I'm so sorry, Miss Myrtle. I had a last minute customer who wanted to talk about my art. I thought I was never going to get the gallery closed."

The older woman smiled at him gently as he walked up the back steps, followed closely by the dog, Buster.

"That's okay. If it was business that made you late, you're forgiven."

Neil handed her the bouquet of fresh flowers and was rewarded with a warm hug from the elderly woman. "Aw, you didn't have to bring me flowers, young man. But they are beautiful and very much appreciated. They'll look lovely on the table." She gestured through the door. "Come on in."

He followed her into the kitchen from where enticing aromas were coming. "Sure does smell good in here."

Neil heard her chuckle.

"Fried chicken. Hope you're hungry."

His stomach gave out a low growl in response and he grinned sheepishly at her. "Guess I am a little hungry. Lunch was a long time ago."

Just then, he heard footsteps coming toward the kitchen doorway which he knew led into the dining room and the rest of the house. Wondering who else Miss Myrtle may have invited, he turned in that direction.

∧∧∧∧∧

Carrie placed the last piece of silverware on the beautiful lace tablecloth next to Aunt Myrtie's Blue Willow china. As she heard voices coming from the kitchen, she turned to look in that direction. It had already been clear to Carrie that her aunt had invited someone else to dinner seeing as there were three place settings at the table. You didn't have to be a genius to figure out it was probably a man, so she wasn't surprised when one of the voices she heard coming from the kitchen was a deep baritone.

She was astonished though when she started to walk into the kitchen and saw who it was. Neil Johnston stood next to her aunt, watching her place a beautiful bouquet of fresh flowers in one of her antique vases.

"Oh, Carrie. Aren't these beautiful?" Her aunt had the decency to blush a little as Carrie looked in Neil's direction and then gave her aunt a pointed look.

Aunt Myrtle, you are in so much trouble.

"Neil, this is my niece's daughter, Carrie Montgomery. Carrie, this is Neil Johnston, the artist I was telling you about."

Carrie finally looked Neil Johnston in the face and was surprised by a twinkle in his eyes. He gave her a smile. "Miss Montgomery, it is a pleasure to officially meet you." He held out his hand and gently took hold of hers, a pleasant feeling running up her arm at the contact.

"Mr. Johnston," Carrie said, the smile on her face feeling stiff. "I believe we've already met—although not 'officially', as you called it."

Aunt Myrtle looked from one to the other with a look of confusion on her face. "I don't understand. What are you two talking about?"

Neil chuckled and thankfully released Carrie's hand. His close proximity totally upset her senses. "Your niece actually visited my gallery this morning. But, of course, I didn't know who she was at the time."

Carrie gave him a friendlier smile, and then turned back to her aunt. "You were right, Aunt Myrtie. It is a beautiful gallery. I even bought a reproduction of one of his paintings."

Her aunt looked back and forth between the two of them, a bemused look on her face. "Did you now? How about that?"

Neil and Carrie gazed at each other for a moment, then both turned back to Aunt Myrtle as if looking for some direction for what to do next. It wasn't long and she was giving each of them tasks. Carrie was instructed to put the vase of flowers on the table, and Neil was given the job of pouring the ice tea into the crystal glasses she'd chosen to use. In a few more minutes everything was ready and all three of them readied to sit around the antique dining room table. Aunt Myrtie removed her floral apron before she sat down, then took a deep breath and turned to Neil.

"Neil, would you please be so kind as to bless the food?"

"I'd be happy to, Miss Myrtie."

Carrie dropped her head and closed her eyes, feeling uncomfortable; not because of the request for prayer as much as being in the presence of the man who was going to pray. Neil Johnston was very attractive, but there was something more in his eyes that drew her to him and that frightened her.

"Lord, thank you for this food on the table before us and the loving hands that prepared it. Please bless this house and the gracious lady who lives here, and especially bless the visitor in our midst. We are eternally grateful to you for all the blessings you give us each and every day, and especially for your eternal love. We ask all these things in Jesus' name, Amen."

Carrie mumbled a quick 'amen' and raised her eyes to find Neil Johnston's dark brown eyes staring across the table at her. Thankfully, he quickly turned away though as Aunt Myrtie handed him a platter loaded with her tasty fried chicken.

It wasn't long and everyone had their plates loaded with the good food and Carrie finally felt herself relaxing a little bit. She was still annoyed with her aunt for inviting this man to share their first formal dinner together, but it was her house after all, so she had the right to invite whomever she wanted. She just hoped her aunt wasn't trying to play matchmaker. Carrie certainly wasn't in the market for a romantic relationship with anyone right now; not after what she had just been through.

She remained quiet as she listened to the other two chat while they ate. She occasionally answered a question if directed at her—but mostly she just ate her food and listened. She'd discovered long ago that the best way to find out what a person was really like was to listen to what they had to say and how they said it. So far it appeared Mr. Neil Johnston was a decent man who genuinely cared about her aunt. He was solicitous, congenial, and polite to both of them; almost too good to be true. It was obvious though that Aunt Myrtie cared about him a great deal, and she mentioned several times in conversation how much she appreciated several things he had done for her at the farm over the past few months.

Suddenly she realized the other two people at the table were looking at her in expectation, and felt her cheeks warm in embarrassment as she wondered what she'd missed in the conversation.

"You didn't hear the question, did you?" Aunt Myrtle asked with a grin sweeping across her face.

Carrie chewed the last bite of her dessert. "I'm so sorry, Aunt Myrtie. Guess I was wool-gathering, as Uncle Jasper used to call it."

Aunt Myrtle chuckled. "You need to apologize to Neil, dear. Not to me."

Carrie looked across the table at Neil who has looking at her with a mischievous smile on his face, the eyebrow over his right eye raised in question.

She felt the heat of embarrassment sweep over her face and knew it had to be turning pink. "Sorry."

He just kept smiling at her. "That's okay; I can repeat the question. I asked if you would like to go to the Cove with me tomorrow morning. I need to take some more photos, and I thought you might like to ride along."

She swallowed hard and looked at her aunt, who had an encouraging look on her face.

"I would feel so much better knowing you weren't going by yourself, Carrie. It's not like it used to be out there. There are a lot more tourists and outsiders around—and not all of them are good people."

Carrie let out a sigh and forced a smile to her face. She really did want to go see the Cove, and she was positive her aunt had her best interests at heart. Carrie, more than most people, was very well aware that not everyone in the world was good. Maybe it was wise to have someone go along with her—at least this time. She looked up from her plate to see Neil still looking at her expectantly, waiting patiently for her answer.

"Sure, that would be great. What time do you want to leave?"

She was rewarded with a huge smile sweeping over Neil's face that made his brown eyes shine. "How about I pick you up about seven thirty? That will give a chance for most of the fog to burn off in the valley, yet still get us there before the Loop gets too busy. Will that work for you or that too early?"

Carrie nodded her agreement, and then glanced over at her aunt. "That's fine. But are you sure I shouldn't come to the restaurant to help you instead, Aunt Myrtle?"

Aunt Myrtie stood up and picked up a few dirty dishes. "You are here to relax, young lady. Not to work for me. Later in the summer, I'll put you to work. Right now just enjoy yourself and spend some time in the mountain air. It will do you a world of good."

Carrie gave her aunt a weak smile. "Yes, ma'am." Then she turned back to look Neil Johnston in the face. "I'll be ready," then added with a little grin, "and if you're lucky, I'll even bring along lunch for us."

A look of surprise crossed his face. "Great. If we have lunch with us, then we can spend as much time there as we want."

Carrie wasn't sure she wanted to spend a great deal of time with this man she knew nothing about, but it would be great to see the Cove again—which was, as far as she was concerned, the most beautiful place on earth.

CHAPTER 5

Neil Johnston drove his Jeep up the narrow, steep gravel drive to the cabin where Myrtle Meyers had told him Carrie was staying. When he made the final turn and the rustic looking log cabin came into view, he let out a low whistle. This was definitely an original log cabin—not one of those kit built cabins. And it had been here a while.

Before he even had time to get out of his vehicle, Carrie came bounding out the front door carrying her purse and a cooler, her camera hanging around her neck by a strap. She was comfortably dressed in blue jeans and a short-sleeved blue denim shirt, with what looked like a flannel shirt thrown over her arm. He was also pleased to see she was wearing hiking shoes instead of those little canvas tennis shoes so many women wore. If they decided to do any walking at all, hiking shoes would be much safer for her.

"Good morning," he called to her as he walked over to join her on the front porch of the cabin.

Today her beautiful blond hair was pulled back into two braids—one on each side, making the cheekbones of her face stand out even more than usual—and as she turned to face him, her blue eyes were as clear as a lake on a calm day.

"Good morning, Mr. Johnston."

He grinned at the stubborn set of her shoulders when he tried to take the cooler from her and was rewarded with a shake of her head as she walked down the steps.

"If we're going to spend the day together, wouldn't it be easier if you call me Neil?" he called after her.

He hurried so he'd get to the Jeep ahead of her, then opened the rear door, allowing her to put the cooler inside. After placing it on the back seat, she brushed past where he stood holding the door open. Neil couldn't help but notice how good she smelled—like fresh air and coconuts.

"I suppose," she mumbled as she moved past him to get in the passenger side of the Jeep.

Neil grinned at her response, pushed the back car door shut, and got in the driver's seat. Miss Myrtie's niece was going to be a hard nut to crack. He didn't know what her problem was, but he wasn't going to let it ruin the day for him. The weatherman was predicting a lovely clear day, and he was headed into the Cove with a beautiful woman at his side. Life was good.

He slowly drove the Jeep down the steep lane and the dirt road through Myrtle's farmland that took them back to the main road, then through town so they could catch Laurel Creek Road which would take them into the Cove. For a time, Neil thought about trying to start a conversation with Carrie, but then decided to let her pout. He didn't know what her problem was, but it was too nice a day for him to let anyone spoil it.

As they entered the northeast end of the Cades Cove part of the Smoky Mountains National Park, Neil slowed down to the posted speed limit of twenty miles per hour. Many of the tourists drove the eleven mile loop so fast he didn't know how they could see anything, but he planned on driving slow and stopping whenever Carrie wanted to—assuming she would eventually decide to talk to him.

"So, how long did you say it had been since you'd been here?"

She finally turned her face away from the window to glance across the seat at him. "About fifteen years."

He nodded. That was a long time ago. She must have only been twelve or thirteen years old the last time she was here.

"It was the summer Uncle Jasper died," she added quietly. "That was the last time I came and spent the summer with him and Aunt Myrtle. Then I started high school and became involved with my friends, and then I went away to college...." Her voice drifted away. "I can't believe I waited so long to come back."

He heard her take a deep breath before exhaling.

"So, Mr. Johnston—Neil—how long have you lived here?"

He smiled. At least they were now on a first name basis. That was a start. And if he had to talk about himself to make her feel more comfortable around him, he could do that. Maybe if he shared about his life, she would share something about hers.

"I've been here about three years. I came here for a vacation one spring and fell in love with the area, so I stayed." He glanced through the front windshield of the vehicle as the woods closed in on both sides of them. "I've never been sorry."

"Have you always been an artist?"

Neil chuckled. "Nope. After college I worked in Chicago at a huge law firm."

She turned a little in the seat to look at him and he tried unsuccessfully to keep his lips from turning up in a smile. It looked like she was finally warming up to him. Maybe this day wouldn't be a total waste after all.

"Really? A lawyer, huh? So why did you leave what sounds like a great job to come here?"

Neil looked at the road ahead of him and tried to decide how to best answer her. He'd been so stressed out when he had first visited here. And his heart had been numbed by the intense pain of loss. Then his eyes had fallen on the beauty of the mountains around him and he had felt hope again. Coming here had healed his heart and brought him to life again; and it was here where he'd decided to take a chance on following his dream of painting.

"I stayed here to do what I've wanted to do my whole life. Paint," he finally answered.

He could have said more, but that was all he was going to share with her at this point. Whatever she was going through, she didn't need to hear about the ghosts of his past that still haunted him.

They were nearing one of Neil's favorite spots in the first part of the Cove, so he slowed down and then finally stopped when he glanced in his rear view mirror long enough to know there was no one coming behind them. He wanted Carrie to have a good view. To the left of the lane was a barbed wire fence, and on the other side of that fence was a wide open field with the morning mists floating across the countryside like a low-lying cloud. The morning sun was just clearing the tops of the mountains and almost glowed as it swept across the land. Neil heard Carrie's excited gasp.

"Oh look, Neil. Look! There are about six deer grazing in the field."

Neil had already seen the deer and wanted to watch Carrie's reaction to seeing them. He wasn't disappointed. It was like watching the excitement of a little girl at Christmas time when she opened a package to find the very doll she'd been wishing for.

"Oh! There are about a dozen wild turkeys too." She turned to look at him, her blue eyes wide and sparkling. "Do you see them, Neil?"

He nodded and smiled, then turned his eyes from the wildlife to watch her watch the turkeys and deer. "Yes, I see them," he almost whispered. It was so much more enjoyable seeing the Cove through her eyes. He loved it here and was looking forward to being able to share it with someone else.

They stayed parked there and watched the scene in the field a few moments longer before Neil finally put his Jeep into gear and moved on down the lane. There was much more to see and he wanted to avoid being in the Cove later in the day when he knew the big crowds would arrive.

It was silent between them the next few minutes as Neil drove down the road that took them deeper through the surrounding woods and fields into the park. It didn't matter how many times Neil came here, the views never got old. Every curve, every hill, brought another beautiful piece of scenery out the car window.

Just a little further down the road he pulled off to the right and parked in a small parking area. "Up for a little walk?"

He was surprised when she turned to him with a big smile on her face and a sparkle in her blue eyes. "John Oliver's place. You bet!"

She was out of the car before Neil could even grab his camera from the back seat. He hurried to catch up with her as she entered the path through the woods that would take them to the John Oliver cabin, one of the original log cabins that were a part of the historic preservation portion of the Park.

Neil couldn't stop the smile spreading across his face. She remembered a lot more about the Cove than she had led him to originally believe—and it was obvious Miss Montgomery was becoming more excited about this trip with every mile.

∧∧∧∧∧

Carrie walked briskly down the dirt path that led through the woods to the first historic building on the Cades Cove Loop. The early morning smell of heavy dew and spring wildflowers swept over her and she let out a sigh of contentment as a feeling of peace swept over her—a peace she hadn't felt in an extremely long time.

It had been a good thing to come here to the Smokies, and this trip back to the Cove was an especially excellent idea. She hadn't been here since she was a young teenager and it had always been one of her favorite spots in the entire world. She just wasn't sure it had been wise to come here with Neil Johnston. It was too soon to know if she could trust the man or not—although her Aunt Myrtle seemed to put a lot of stock in him—and he seemed nice enough. She was just having a difficult time trusting any man right now. But until he gave her a reason to worry, she was going to enjoy herself.

Carrie glanced behind her and then slowed down a little as she realized Neil was behind her on the trail.

"Sorry. I tend to walk fast."

She heard Neil's chuckle as his long legs quickly caught up with her. "I noticed."

"I love it here," she said quietly as he joined her and they briskly walked down the path. "There isn't another place like it anywhere in the world."

"I totally agree. That is why I moved here."

Carrie took a moment to look over at the man walking next to her. Even though he had the strap of his expensive camera draped around his neck, he didn't look to her like what she thought an artist/photographer would look like. She wasn't one to normally stereotype people, but Neil Johnston looked more like he belonged in these mountains than most men she knew would. Today he wore faded blue jeans which she noticed he filled out very nicely. It also looked like he worked out or got plenty of exercise as the light gray, long sleeved tee-shirt he wore couldn't hide his broad muscular shoulders and arms. A day's or more worth of whiskers gave his face a rustic look, and his brown wavy hair was a little longer than most men in the city would wear it; but it looked good on him. Neil Johnston was definitely easy on the eyes.

She bit her lip and gave her head a little shake. Even though he was attractive to look at, she wasn't interested in getting involved with a man right now—any man.

As the Cove's first historic building on the loop came into sight up ahead, Carrie turned her attention to it. Everything looked exactly as she remembered from her childhood, with the cabin nestled at the base of the mountains and the woods directly behind it. Split rail fences surrounded the small one room cabin with little covered porches at the front and the back and a huge stone fireplace built at one end. She was a little disappointed to see a couple of other early-rising people had arrived ahead of them, along with a park ranger who she could hear, telling the couple the history of the cabin. She had selfishly hoped she and Neil would be able to go through the Cove by themselves without other people around—more like it had been when she was a child. But the public had discovered what a beautiful place it was, and now the tourists flocked here by the millions. That made her doubly glad Neil had suggested coming early.

"You'll notice this cabin has notched corners so it needs no nails or pegs to hold it together," the uniformed park ranger stated, his hands pointing to the corner of the cabin. "Gravity holds the logs together." He and a young couple stood on the front porch of the cabin and Carrie and Neil made their way across the yard and slowly walked up the steps to join them.

"And as you can see, this stone chimney is held together with mud mortar," the ranger continued as he led them into the cabin.

It was dark inside the small building, and it took a moment for Carrie's eyes to adjust after being outside in the bright sunlight. The interior was as she remembered; empty of any furnishings, but plainly showing the workmanship of the cabin.

"John Oliver and his wife came to the Cove in the early 1800's. He was the first permanent white settler here," the park ranger added.

Carrie reached out to lightly touch the framework of the eight-paned window in the corner of the cabin near where she stood. The view outside the window was breathtaking. Through the glass panes she saw an open meadow of greening field grass with woods on both sides and a clear view of the blue/green mountains rising in the distance. What a stunning sight this would be to wake up to each day; although, she couldn't even begin to imagine living in this confined one-room cabin with all your children, year in-year out. It had to have been tough.

"This cabin isn't their original homestead though, is it?" Carrie asked.

The park ranger, the other couple, and Neil, all turned to look at her in surprise, and she felt the heat of embarrassment on her face when she realized she'd voiced her thoughts out loud. Then the park ranger, who had introduced himself as Will, smiled at her and nodded his head.

"You know your stuff, young lady. As a matter of fact, the original Oliver cabin stood about fifty yards behind this cabin. This one was actually what they called the honeymoon house, and they built it for their son to use when he married."

Carrie gave the ranger a little smile, thankful he had made her feel at ease after her unintentionally blurting out her question. Sometimes she didn't know when to keep her mouth shut.

While the ranger went back to talking to the other couple about the cabin and explaining about the upstairs loft which was reached by going up a narrow steep staircase, Carrie walked across the small room toward the back door. She sensed more than saw Neil follow her as she stepped across the doorsill onto another small covered porch. Carrie paused for a moment and gazed across the yard and into the hills and the woods behind the cabin. She could see several different kinds of ferns and wildflowers growing in the wooded area behind the homestead. Carrie recognized wild Trillium, Dutchmen's Breeches, and Columbine. Unfortunately, it was too early in the year for many of the wildflowers that would later fill the fields and forests.

As she stepped off the rough-cut plank porch and into the grass, tiny droplets of moisture still clung to the grasses from the morning mists. Even though she was wearing her hiking boots, she could feel the dampness swirling around her ankles. She took a deep breath of the early morning air and knew she had a smile of happiness on her face. This place had always meant so much to her.

It felt so good to be back.

"You know a great deal more about this place than you've led me to believe," Neil said softly as he walked up next to her.

She turned and gave him a little smile. He'd been nice enough to bring her here; she guessed she owed him a little explanation.

"When I was a kid, Uncle Jasper and Aunt Myrtie spent as much time here in the Cove as they could, showing me everything and telling me stories of their own families living and growing up here. We used to have picnics in the fields and spent hours walking around looking at everything. I guess I didn't realize how much of it I still remembered—or how much I missed it. I love being back here."

Carrie glanced over to see Neil gazing at her, a smile on his face and kindness in his brown eyes. The more time she spent with this man, the more comfortable she was coming to feel around him.

"Hopefully you'll share some of their stories with me sometime. I love to get the real stories of the places I paint and photograph."

She gave a nervous laugh. "If you've visited the Cove as often as you said you have, I'm sure the rangers have filled you in on everything there is to know."

A few moments later Carrie strode around to the front of the cabin, knowing Neil would follow her. She felt bad for pushing him away when he was making a real effort to be friends. She let out a sigh and turned to get another view of the mountains from this viewpoint, then pulled out her camera to take a couple of photos before starting back down the trail toward Neil's car.

She just didn't know when or if she'd ever feel she could trust a man again.

CHAPTER 6

Neil followed Carrie back to the small parking area where they'd left his vehicle. Once they were both inside the Jeep, he drove out of the lot and followed the paved road back through the mountains. The next stops were two of the Cove's churches. Neil was excited when they arrived at the Primitive Baptist Church, which was his favorite of all the Cove's churches. With its wide cedar plank floors, walls, and ceilings, you could smell the cedar as soon as you walked into the old structure. Two rows of pews sat on each side of the building facing the altar, with two more short rows turned inward on both sides near the front.

There was a metal plate in the floor in the center of the aisle near the front. Neil guessed at one time it was the location of a wood stove, which would have been the only way to heat this old building. He remembered from the concrete marker at the front of the building that the church was established in 1827, but if he recalled his information correctly, this particular building was built around 1887. Regardless, the building was over a hundred years old, but was very well preserved by the Park. Thankfully, in this building there was no park ranger, so Carrie and he had the place to themselves.

Neil took several camera shots of sunlight pouring through the multi-paned windows as it hit one of the roughly-built wooden pews. Even though it was the plainest and most rustic of all the churches in the Park, he still preferred this church over the others. Perhaps it was the very plainness that drew him to it. It was a peaceful building with a feeling of holiness to it and it always gave him comfort to be here.

He watched Carrie take a seat in one of the pews near the back and thought perhaps she was praying, so left her alone. She sat quietly, staring at the front of the church and its simple raised altar where a Bible sat. Not being able to resist, he took a few shots of her. He knew she would never give him permission to sell them, so he would keep them for his own collection. And that was okay with him. He just wanted to have some reminders of this day with her.

Carrie Montgomery wasn't anything like he had expected when Miss Myrtie told him her niece was here from the city. He had expected a woman more like the ones he had known in Chicago. Those women had been career-driven individuals—cold and brittle in their relationships, and difficult to be around. Carrie, on the other hand, seemed almost fragile and vulnerable on every level. There was strength in her eyes though, and he couldn't help but wonder what she had been through to make her the person she was. He was sure she had a story to tell. He just wasn't sure she would ever warm up to him enough to share it with him.

He watched her stand from the pew and walk toward him, a definite twinkle in her eyes. She pointed up at the ceiling and his eyes followed the direction of her hand.

"Did anyone ever explain to you about the handprints on the ceiling and how they got there?"

Neil gazed up at the wide cedar boards that made up the ceiling and easily found the prints she was point to. He shook his head and gave her a grin. He could feel a story coming.

"The men that built this church used green lumber and because the sap was wet, you can still see some of their fingerprints on the boards."

Turning his lens to the ceiling, Neil zoomed in and snapped a couple of photos of the areas she pointed out. He couldn't believe that sometime during one of his many visits to this place no one had ever shown him the handprints. Just one more surprise from Carrie Montgomery.

She turned from where she stood in front of him and walked out the door of the church and down the gravel path at the side of the building toward the small cemetery behind the church. He quickly followed, feeling almost as if she was on a quest to find her past and he was just along for the ride. That was okay with him. Hopefully it would give him a chance to know her better, and maybe he could help her find whatever it was she was searching for.

They strolled through the old graveyard, the only noise the quiet crunch of their footsteps on the gravel path, and the muted sounds of the song birds in the trees around them. The sun had risen and burned off most of the morning mists, and the sky had turned to a beautiful, clear azure blue. It was going to be a lovely day, and the warmth from the sun beating down on his back felt good.

He watched Carrie stroll slowly down the path a ways and then pause in front of a grouping of small stones. She kneeled down and gently brushed old grass clippings and leaves away from them. Putting his camera to his eye, he snapped a couple of quick photos, hoping to catch the way the sunlight made her blond hair glow.

Neil was trying not to be, but he was fascinated with watching the young woman before him. After being absent from this area for so many years, it was touching to watch her reaction to seeing the Cove again. It was obvious this place meant a great deal to her, which left him confused. Why hadn't she ever come back before this?

Carrie turned to look at him—thankfully after he'd already dropped the camera back to his chest.

"My great-grandparents are buried here," she stated softly.

He walked over to squat down next to her, catching a whiff of her shampoo. Her hair smelled like coconut. She smelled good, and for a moment Neil wondered what it would be like to be even closer to her, maybe even hold her in his arms. Then he took a deep breath and let it out. They were together today as friends. Nothing more. What was he thinking?

"Do you remember them?" he finally asked in a whisper, not wanting to shatter the silence of the moment.

Carrie shook her head. "All I have are the stories my parents and aunts and uncles told me about them. I'm thinking about compiling it into a booklet about their history though—while Aunt Myrtie is still around to help me recall all the old stories. I'd hate to lose them. I know there are some she knows that I don't even remember."

Neil nodded. "That's a great idea, Carrie. And if you need photos of this area for your book, I have oodles of them." He grinned over at her. "I've taken thousands of photos in the Cove over the years."

He was rewarded with her finally smiling back at him and Neil felt an unexpected tug at his heart. She was a beautiful woman, but when she smiled, she was absolutely gorgeous.

As they both stood and he watched as she brushed last year's dead leaves from her knees, she looked over at him again, her lips upturned a little grin and an unexpected blatantly mischievous look replaced the previous sadness he had seen in her eyes.

"So, what do you think, Mr. Johnston; are you up for some hiking?"

He followed her as she headed down the path and back to his car. Miss Carrie Montgomery had something planned next on their itinerary, and he wasn't sure he wanted to know what it was.

Neil opened the Jeep's passenger side door for her and then stood at the side of the car for a moment after she got in and looked down at her. Okay, he'd play along with her.

"How long a hike are we talking here?"

She grinned up at him standing there. "Let's stop at the Elijah Oliver place and we can talk about it."

He chuckled, shut the car door, and then jogged over to the driver's side and got in. It was starting to appear like Carrie was thawing out a little bit toward him, and he kind of liked the idea. Neil tried to avoid the thought that he was attracted to her as anything other than Miss Myrtle's niece. It looked like she had some baggage in her past she had to deal with, and he had plenty of his own. Friendship was all he wanted and was certainly all he could offer her at this point in his life.

They didn't bother stopping at the next two churches as both of them had seen them before. And if Neil had his way, this was only the first of what he hoped would be many trips back to the Cove with Carrie Montgomery. He couldn't remember a time when he'd enjoyed himself so much. He'd spent far too much time alone, and it was fun to have someone else along for the ride—somebody who appreciated this beautiful place as much as he did.

They drove slowly down the Loop road toward the other Oliver place, Neil turning frequently to watch Carrie's face as they wound around another curve only to spot another set of mountain ranges or another flock of wild turkeys or deer grazing in the fields. They even spotted a mama bear and a couple of her cubs, scurrying across an open field. When Carrie caught sight of them, her face really lit up. It made him feel good to know she was enjoying herself so much. Not every woman he knew would get excited about seeing nothing but nature and wildlife all around them. Face it, other than his wonderful wife that he had lost, most of the women from his past were selfish and self-centered and would never have even considered coming to a place like this. And even Lisa wouldn't have appreciated all the nature of the Cove. She was too much of a city gal.

Neil did stop the Jeep once to pull over at a turnoff when he saw what looked like a Northern Harrier in a field. He couldn't pass up a photo opportunity like that. He waited patiently as it flew above them and then came down to land in the open land before him, and his perseverance finally paid off when he was able to get several great shots of the bird. He'd been trying to catch it on film for months.

So far, it appeared this was going to be a good day for him.

A little further down the Loop Road, Carrie asked him to stop briefly when there was a narrow place for him to pull over. She exited the car and he watched as she walked back a short distance to a heavily treed area with the remains of a few late daffodils. He knew because of the appearance of the flowers that this had once been a homestead, even though any remains of a cabin or house were long gone. He remained behind in the car, somehow understanding that for whatever reason, Carrie needed a few minutes alone in this particular spot, so he gave her all the time she needed. He did keep his eyes peeled for any bears and the many other varieties of wildlife that he knew were all around them.

He'd seen the black bears that lived in the Cove many times during his trips there, but he'd always been very careful to stay away from them. The park authorities warned people constantly about leaving the bears alone and to avoid getting anywhere near them. They were wild animals and these woods and mountains were their habitat—their home. People needed to realize that and leave them alone. There was nothing more lethal than a mother bear protecting her cubs. They were fun to watch from a distance, and Neil had even been fortunate enough to get some great photos of them over the years using a high powered zoom lens, but he knew well enough to stay away from them. Some people were idiots though and thought they could treat them like pets—some even tried to feed them. Neil knew they were far from being domesticated creatures, but instead were powerful and dangerous animals and it was best to keep your distance.

After a few moments, Carrie came back to the Jeep, her head down and her eyes not looking at him as she got in and shut the passenger side door. He wondered for a minute or two if she were angry with him and wracked his brain while he tried to figure out what he'd done to upset her.

They'd moved on down the road a ways when he finally heard her sigh.

"Thanks for stopping for me. That was where my great-grandparents' homestead used to be."

He glanced across the car at her. So that was why she'd acted the way she had when she'd come back to the car. It wasn't because she was angry with him; it was because she was affected emotionally by being there. She hadn't been kidding when she had told him her roots went deep here.

"You're welcome," he finally muttered around the lump in his throat. "No problem at all, and if you want to stop anywhere else, just let me know."

She nodded and it was quiet between them until they came to the next cabin on the historic list; the Elijah Oliver cabin. Neil wondered if she knew much about this one. He decided after the last few somber minutes to try and lighten the mood.

"So, Miss Cades Cove Tour Guide, what can you tell me about this place?"

He was rewarded with a grin on her face when she turned to him. "Well, how much do ya want to know, City Boy?"

Neil laughed and after he parked in the lot, then followed her as she got out of the car and started down the trail.

Once they reached the old cabin, Carrie took her 'tour guide' pose, placing her left hand on her hip, and pointing with her right hand toward the rustic cabin. "Elijah Oliver was the son of John Oliver, whose cabin we visited earlier—and this was his place after he married. After the Civil War he and his family moved back here to the Cove. If you look at the front of this particular cabin, you will notice it has what's called a 'strangers room' built on the front porch. Mr. Oliver was a very charitable man—he was in fact a deacon in his church—and if a stranger came to his door needing shelter for the evening, he graciously provided it, along with a hot meal."

"He was actually a good friend of my great-grandfather," she added in her normal voice.

Neil grinned as he watched her walk down the gravel path toward the front porch of the cabin. It was like listening to a real tour guide. She should get a job for the Park Service.

"Is there anything you don't know about the Cove?"

She turned to look back at him and laughed her musical laugh again. "Nope."

He shook his head and followed her, happy he'd been able to lift her mood again. She'd seemed so sad after they'd left her ancestors' old place and it had saddened him to see her that way. Fortunately, she had gone along with him when he'd asked her to play tour guide and it had appeared to cheer her up.

They spent some time investigating the old cabin and Neil took a few more photos of her and the cabin, along with some white trillium wildflowers blossoming in the wooded area out back. Then they returned to the car and he drove a little further down the road as she gave him directions to turn to the right and drive down a narrow lane between fenced in fields to what looked like another parking area.

"This is it," she said as he parked his Jeep in a parking spot next to a couple of other vehicles.

"This is what?"

She smiled over at him. "Are you up for that hike I mentioned earlier?"

"You asked me that before. How far?"

"It's two and a half miles in, and two and a half miles back. But trust me, it's worth it to see Abrams Falls."

Neil nodded. He'd heard about the Falls, but had never taken the time to make the hike. But if Carrie wanted to go, he was game.

"Sure, why not?"

She grinned at him. "Good. And because you're being such a good sport, I've brought lunch for us to eat when we get there."

He followed her as she got out of the car and left the parking area to enter a path through the forest. The other people didn't appear to be going on the hike and were just wandering around the area, snapping photos with their cheap cameras. Deep in his heart, Neil privately hoped the others would leave and not follow Carrie and him on the trail. It would be nice if they could have the place to themselves just a little longer.

As they passed a wooden sign that said 'Abrams Falls Trailhead; moderately difficult 3-4 hour hike', Neil wondered what he had gotten himself into. He also wondered what 'moderately difficult' meant to the person who made the sign. He liked to think he was in pretty good shape, but it had been a long time since he'd climbed any mountains.

Carrie and he crossed a wooden bridge and took the path to the left which led toward the Falls. They strolled along the trail cut into the side of the hillside—the creek gurgling beside them on one side and the shade of the woods all around them on the other. The trees were teaming with birds' songs and since the sun had burned off the early morning mist, it had warmed up into a beautiful day. Neil took a deep breath of the mountain air. He had a lovely woman at his side and he was tramping through some of the most gorgeous countryside in the world.

God was good.

Along the way, Carrie shared what she knew about the Creek and Abram Falls.

"Abrams Falls is named after a Cherokee Chief, Oskuah, who took the name of Abraham."

Neil watched the young woman beside him in amazement as she nimbly traversed the hiking trail which weaved up and down and back and forth along the ridges surrounding Cades Cove. She talked occasionally to Neil, pointing out a particular wildflower along the path, or a squirrel or some other wildlife in the woods. They stopped several times so he could take photos, and he was very appreciative of her patience while he wandered around to get just the right light before he took the shot.

They took turns carrying the lunch cooler, although Neil wanted to just take it from her—him being the man and everything. But Miss Montgomery had an independent streak like her great-aunt, and insisted on taking her turn. It was a long walk for Neil who wasn't used to so much physical activity, but very enjoyable with the river flowing along beside them. And even though he knew he would feel it in his muscles the next day, he was extremely glad he'd decided to come. He was getting the opportunity to see a side of these mountains he'd never seen before.

Carrie's voice brought him back to the present. "Eighteen small streams that come down from the mountains empty into Abrams Creek," she said. "We've had some rain the last couple of weeks, so the water level is higher than it would be if you were here in late July or August."

She looked over at him as if to gauge how he was holding up. "We're almost there. This is Arbutus Ridge we've been climbing."

Neil nodded. He had assumed they were getting close as he'd started hearing the roar of the falls a ways back.

She took a trail to the right and crossed a very narrow foot bridge across a small stream with Neil following closely behind. "This is Wilson Creek, and..." she said as she turned to the left and walked through a rocky wooded area, "there it is."

Neil followed her as they climbed over the rocks which took them to the side of the pool surrounding the Falls. Lush green ferns grew on the shady banks of the creek, and the sun filtered down through the treetops above them. He stood next to Carrie and looked at the power of the water falling over the rocks in a twenty-foot plunge. Below the falls was a deep pool of churning water with a mist floating up from the water which caused a cool moisture in the surrounding air.

It was spectacular.

He looked over at the woman beside him and smiled. "Wow. Thanks for bringing me here, Carrie. It's beautiful."

She nodded. "I thought you might like it." She pointed in the direction of the falls. "Get out your camera and take your photos and I'm going to find a spot for us to eat our lunch." She pointed toward the rocks along the side of the water. "Just be careful though. The rocks can be very slippery with the moss and the mist in the air."

He smiled at her words of caution. She sounded like a teacher—or a mother. "Yes, ma'am," he said as he saluted her and watched as she turned away with the lunch cooler.

Neil was able to get some great photos of the falls and the nearby woods. The sun was high in the sky and he loved the way the light filtered down through the surrounding trees. To make the place even more special, they had it entirely to themselves. He assumed later in the day, especially in the summer when the weather warmed, this part of the park would be much busier and people would be swarming over these trails and rocks. Right now though, it was just the two of them.

A short time later Carrie called him over to a flat rocky area away from the pool where she had thrown down a blanket and spread out the items from the cooler. He smiled as it became obvious she had put some time into organizing this. It made him feel good to know she had planned something special like this for him. When he had picked her up that morning at her house, he hadn't been sure what her feelings were about going anywhere with him. The night before it had seemed more like she was agreeing to the trip just to make her aunt happy. It had made him feel rather uncomfortable when Myrtle had more or less forced her into accepting his offer.

"Would you bless the food, Neil?" she asked him after they both sat down on the blanket.

Neil gave a short prayer of thanks for the food and eagerly accepted the heavy paper plate Carrie had loaded down with food. There was a huge stack of thinly sliced turkey and cheese on what looked like thick slices of homemade bread. When he took a bite, Neil almost groaned in appreciation as the taste of tangy mustard and mayonnaise hit his taste buds. There was also an ample helping of potato salad on his plate along with several deviled eggs. It was good food.

"Did you make all this, Carrie?"

∧∧∧∧∧

Carrie finished chewing and then swallowed a bite of her potato salad and smiled across the blanket at the man who'd asked the question. He sounded surprised as he asked the question.

"Yes, I did."

She gave a little chuckle when she heard what sounded like a murmur of enjoyment as he took another bite of his sandwich.

"This is really good." He grinned at her around his sandwich. "Did you learn how to cook from your Aunt Myrtle?"

Carrie nodded as she finished chewing a bite of her own sandwich. "Some. Also my mom and grandma. The women in my family all know how to cook—and bake." She pulled another plastic container out of the cooler. "I hope you like apple pie."

Neil groaned at her and Carrie couldn't help but giggle a little. She couldn't believe how good it made her feel to have someone enjoy her cooking. She hadn't cooked for anyone since she and Sean had quit seeing each other, so other than her friend, Ashlynn, no one else had enjoyed her cooking for quite a while. She used to enjoy cooking and baking for her family back when she still lived at home with her parents. And Sean had preferred going out to some fancy restaurant rather than stay at home and have her cook for him.

"So," the man across the blanket from her said. "Tell me a little about yourself, Carrie Montgomery. What brings you to this neck of the woods this summer—other than to visit your Aunt Myrtle?"

Carrie felt the smile leave her face and she struggled to swallow the food she'd been chewing. She had known that question was coming eventually. People always wanted to know about you—what you did for a living—what your life was like back home.

Her therapist back in Lexington had told her she needed to open up about the attack and talk to people more about it—share what had happened to her in the hopes it would help others. But was Neil Johnston someone she could share it with? She didn't really know the man at all. All she knew was he was a good friend of her aunt's, and his eyes staring at her across the blanket were filled with obvious compassion—like he really cared about her answer. Maybe now was the time to share her story. Was he the person she could talk to about it? She sighed. She felt more comfortable with this man she'd just met than she had around any friend—male or female—for years. She'd been praying for a friend to help her through this; perhaps this was God answering her prayer.

"I'm not sure I can talk about it, Neil," she finally said. "And even if I could, I'm not sure you want to hear it. It's not a pretty story."

She saw him put down his sandwich and gaze at her for a few seconds. "You don't have to if you don't want to, Carrie. But if you feel like you need to talk about whatever it is, I've been told I'm a good listener."

Carrie looked down at her half-eaten meal and suddenly didn't feel very hungry anymore. Then she looked back up at the man before her. Maybe it was where they were—secluded and safe here in the mountains with only nature around them. She didn't understand why, but she felt like she was supposed to tell him her story.

"Maybe it's time." She took a deep breath for courage and then exhaled the breath slowly.

It was more difficult than she thought to talk about it with a total stranger. Telling her parents had been gut-wrenching, but she'd tried to spare them all the details. Going through it all with the therapist and again at the trial, the only way she'd been able to do it was to recite the details as if she were talking about it happening to someone else.

This time, it seemed more personal.

"I had to take a medical leave from my job. I was having panic attacks and kept falling apart in front of a classroom filled with second graders. That didn't go over so well with the parents and administration." She swallowed hard. "It probably had something to do with the fact that I was attacked one night in my apartment."

She saw the look of shock and pain cross Neil's face, then waited for the look of disgust she was sure would follow. She had become accustomed to that look that made her feel like she should have been able to stop the man from hurting her. When the look didn't appear, she decided to keep talking. Even though her therapist had explained to her over and over again that she hadn't done anything to encourage the guy to attack her, she still felt like she was somehow to blame.

Carrie dropped her eyes to stare at the small pieces of fabric in the patchwork quilt they were sitting on. It was an old one Neil had gotten out of the back of his Jeep and she let her mind drift for a moment while she wondered who had made it.

"A few years ago, I dated a guy—we only went out a couple of times before I broke it off when I realized he was becoming overly possessive. Then he started to stalk me. I told him to stop, that I wasn't interested in him. But he wouldn't leave me alone." Carrie gulped as the remembered fear came back to her. Then she took a deep breath and gazed out at the Falls. He couldn't hurt her anymore, and it was supposed to be cathartic for her to talk about it—even though it was so difficult.

"One night when I was alone in my apartment, he broke in right after I'd gone to bed. He beat me up pretty bad, and I truly believe his intent was to rape me." She swallowed hard again and dropped her eyes to the blanket. "If my roommate hadn't come home from her date early and surprised him in the act, I'm sure he would have done so and then killed me. I was sure I was going to die that night."

She closed her eyes and tried to bury the grief and fear that threatened to engulf her as her memory replayed the event in her head. Even though she often re-lived the whole incident during her therapy sessions and in her nightmares, Carrie had tried to block out the details of the attack as much as she could—ever since the trial was over. During the trial she had to live it all again and again, and it had almost been her undoing.

"Oh, Carrie," she heard Neil say quietly. "How horrible. No one should have to go through something like that. I am so sorry."

Carrie raised her eyes to his, surprised at the compassion she saw there.

"So, please tell me they caught the guy."

She was surprised by the anger in his voice and took a deep breath before she answered him. "When my roommate came home and found him in my room, she screamed. He punched her, then pushed her down and ran out of the apartment. When he knocked her down, she hit her head against a table and it almost knocked her out, but fortunately, she came back around enough to call 911. I was a mental case by then and couldn't function at all."

The truth was, she had barely been conscious and by the time the paramedics had arrived, had curled into the fetal position, sobbing in fear in a corner of her bedroom. Thank goodness, Ashlynn had been there.

Carrie looked back across the blanket at him. "When the police came, Ashlynn was able to give them a pretty good description of the man, which was a good thing. Even though I recognized his voice, it was so dark in the room I never saw his face. It turned out to be that same guy I had dated for a while."

Carrie paused for a moment. "I'm a school teacher and he'd been stalking me—even after I'd had a restraining order put out against him. He couldn't get to me in the school building during the day, but when I left at night he was always there across the parking lot, standing by his vehicle and just watching me. Even though he never spoke to me or approached me, it totally creeped me out. Then he broke into the apartment."

She gasped at the effort it was taking her to keep from crying. Tears were burning her eyes and she blinked a couple of times to try and clear her vision. Even after all this time, she couldn't talk about it without breaking down.

"While he was attacking me, he kept calling me 'his girl'—kept saying he loved me and wasn't ever going to let me go. The reason I felt he was going to kill me was he had a knife and he kept repeating, if he couldn't have me, no one else could either."

By this time, Carrie was so encompassed by the feelings of that day, she wasn't even thinking about what Neil thought about her story. As she dropped her face into her hands, the fear and pain Lloyd Taylor had caused her returned, and the feeling of being dirty for him having touched her swept over her again. Even though it was a warm day, Carrie shuddered as her high-strung nerves gave way to the experience of reliving it all.

Was she ever going to forget it?

Suddenly she felt strong arms pull her into a standing position and wrap her in a hug. Instead of the fear she expected at the physical contact, she felt comfort from these arms.

While she sobbed into his shirt, she heard Neil Johnston repeat over and over to her the same words, "I'm so sorry, Carrie. I'm so sorry," while he slowly rubbed her back and gently held her in his arms.

Carrie's sobs finally turned into hiccups and she pulled away long enough to wipe the tears from her face with the palms of her hands, feeling embarrassment sweep over her. "I'm so sorry, Neil. I can't believe I fell apart like that. But, I've never told anyone the whole story before—other than the police and my therapist."

He looked down at her with a look on his face she couldn't read. "Then I am honored you chose to share it with me; and you have absolutely nothing to apologize for, Carrie. After what you've been through, I'm surprised you can even talk about it."

She sniffed and stepped away from him, suddenly feeling very self-conscious. Even though she'd talked to the therapist about it many times, she'd never broken down like this in front of him. What was wrong with her? When was she going to get over what had happened to her and become a normal human being again?

Carrie took a deep breath of the fresh air around her and raised her eyes to the sun filtering through the treetops, swiping at her wet face again. "According to statistics, one out of every six women have been stalked; one out of five, raped, and one out of four have been the victim of physical violence. But I have to tell you, Neil, knowing the numbers doesn't make it any easier to live with when you're the one it happens to."

"But he didn't get away with it, right? They got him?"

Carrie nodded and turned to look at Neil again and exhaled a large breath. "They caught him, and he was tried and convicted and put in prison."

She saw Neil's nod and heard the conviction in his voice. "Good."

It was quiet between the two of them for a moment as they both stood there.

"But it's obvious you've never really gotten over what happened to you, have you, Carrie?"

She lifted her eyes to his, reading compassion there, and a shared understanding of the pain of trauma. How could he look like that—like he almost understood her pain?

"No, I haven't." Carrie took another deep breath and sighed. "That's why I'm here for the summer and not finishing out my teaching year. Like I said, I kept falling apart in my classroom in front of my students. The administration frowns on that, and after a couple of complaints from parents, they didn't have any choice but to put me on leave."

She sniffed a little, then reached in her jeans pocket for a tissue to blow her nose. "I keep thinking it will get better. It's been almost a year since it happened. By now I ought to be better, you know?" She gave a bitter laugh. "Even my boyfriend, Sean, finally gave up on me and walked away. I guess I can't blame him. I wasn't much fun to be around."

Carrie saw Neil drop his head and stare at the blanket before him. She wished she knew what was going through his head. While she was telling him her story, he hadn't looked at her like he thought she was crazy, so maybe in some unknown way he really understood what the attack had done to her psyche. No one else seemed to understand.

Even her therapist back in Lexington kept telling her she needed to accept what happened to her and move on.

"It kind of overwhelms an individual's ability to cope, doesn't it?" he finally said quietly.

She looked over at him in surprise. He really did understand.

Carrie finally nodded. "Yes, it does." Then she took another deep breath and straightened her stature. This had to end. She'd cowered in the corner long enough.

"But I'm going to make it. I can't let the fear and anger win. I refuse to let it!"

Again their eyes locked for a moment of understanding, then he motioned in the direction of their food.

"I suppose we should finish our lunch and see if we can find something a little less intense to talk about."

Giving him a weak smile, she nodded and sat back down on the blanket, while he did the same.

When he picked up his almost empty plate of food, she turned back to her sandwich. It was quiet between them for a while and she wondered what he was thinking about. Now that he'd heard the nasty truth about her, he probably found her to be just as disgusting as her boyfriend had. Sean had let her know right away that he couldn't deal with what had happened to her. It had affected her response toward him—she hadn't even been able to let him kiss her or hold her hand—and he'd decided he was tired of dealing with it. So, he'd told her they were through. Just one more thing the attack had taken away from her. She had thought Sean loved her no matter what. But she'd been wrong. Maybe that type of committed love only existed in romance novels and fairy tales.

Carrie took a deep breath of fresh air and exhaled again, trying to steady her nerves. Neil had mentioned discussing more enjoyable things. While she chewed another bite of her potato salad, her mind struggled to come up with something for them to talk about now.

She'd just spilled her guts to him. Maybe he'd be willing to share a little bit about himself with her. It seemed only fair, after all.

The Healing Hills

CHAPTER 7

He wanted to kick himself. He never should have pushed her into talking about her past. Neil had known from the haunted look in her eyes that Carrie had gone through something extremely traumatic, so why had he pressed her? Why hadn't he just let it go? He recognized the painful signs from his own miserable past; but he'd been thinking more in terms of her having lost a job, having a health scare, or maybe a bad breakup with a boyfriend. He'd had no idea of the floodgates of horrible memories he had unleashed in Carrie simply by asking her one little question.

He nibbled on the bite of apple pie he'd taken. It was good; equally as tasty as her aunt's. She was not only beautiful and personable; she was a good cook. She'd make some lucky man out there a wonderful wife. What was the matter with this boyfriend of hers? If he'd really loved her, how could he just walk away from her right when she needed him most? Neil mentally shook himself. He didn't have any right in even thinking about her that way. They hadn't even known each other that long. And yet, there was something about her.... At times it felt like he'd known her forever.

"My family was killed in a car accident four years ago."

Neil didn't even realized he'd spoken the words out loud until her enormous blue eyes turned on him with a look of shock on her face.

"Oh, Neil," she almost whispered.

He swallowed hard, feeling the muscles in his jaws work as he tried to get control of his emotions. He'd talked about the accident dozens of times in the grief counseling sessions he'd sat through right after it happened. It never got any easier for him though. A part of his life had changed that day and he'd lost something he would never be able to get back.

"My wife, Lisa, was driving our family van home from a Mom's Day activity at our church. Our two year old little girl, Kaylee, was in the back seat in her car seat."

He glanced up from his plate briefly to see Carrie's eyes glued on him, then dropped his eyes back to the blanket underneath him. He couldn't look at her right now. If he did, he would lose it. Even though it was difficult to talk about, after what she'd just told him, he felt he owed her. If she could tell him what she had been through, he could tell her about his losses. Maybe there would be some comfort for her in their shared misery.

"An oncoming semi-truck's brakes failed on a curve and the driver lost control of his rig. The tractor trailer swerved over into Lisa's lane and slammed into the side of our van. It rolled three times before wrapping around a tree."

He heard her gasp and he swallowed hard again, carefully placing his plate and fork down on the blanket. He wasn't sure he could eat anything else right now anyway. Just remembering what the van had looked like when he had seen it was enough to make him sick—even though it had been weeks after the accident before he'd been able to face it; long after the funerals.

"They were both killed. Lisa's autopsy showed she died instantly. Kaylee never gained consciousness and died two days later in the hospital."

"I'm so sorry," he felt her touch on his shoulder and suddenly realized sometime while he'd been talking she had walked over to stand behind him.

He took a deep breath. "Thanks. It took me a long time to get over losing them, and a lot of grief counseling."

Carrie gave his shoulder one last squeeze, then walked over and sat back down across from him. "I can't imagine going through something like that," she said quietly.

He grimaced. Like what she had gone through had been easier?

"I don't know if I could have made it without my faith in God," he finally said. "Knowing He was there beside me through it all...." He took a deep breath and exhaled. "Sounds like we've both had our share of heart-aches, Carrie."

He saw her nod slowly before she finally raised her eyes to look at him. Neil didn't have any idea of where she stood spiritually, but he knew from personal experience that his faith that God with him through the whole experience was the only thing that had kept him from losing his sanity right after the accident.

"I guess my point is, Carrie, I've learned that I can let the bad things that happen to me destroy me, or I can choose to embrace them as a part of making me who I am. I truly believe everything happens to us for a reason. I also feel God puts us in certain places at just the right times to be able to help people who have also been through similar experiences. Maybe that's why we're here today," he added.

Neil saw her nod slowly as if letting his words sink in, then she raised her blue eyes to gaze at him. "I'm so sorry you lost your wife and little girl, Neil. I know it wasn't easy talking about it. Thank you for telling me what happened. I had no idea you'd gone through something like that."

He gave her a small smile, instantly feeling better about having to remember it all. "You're welcome. Now that we know what we've both been through, hopefully we can help each other by being there to talk to if we need to. Not everyone understands."

She nodded, and then started picking up their remains of their meal.

"Guess we'd better start the long walk back, huh?"

Carrie looked over at him, a little smile returning to her face. "Yup. So what do you think, city boy? Do you think you can make it?"

He gave a little laugh and it felt good to leave the grief behind. "What choice do I have? I don't think you're big enough to carry both me and that cooler out of here."

Her little laugh was music to his ears. It sounded like she'd been able to put their serious discussion behind her too, and that was very good.

The walk back to the car seemed to take less time than the trip in, but perhaps it was because the two of them had reached an understanding of sorts back at the Falls. On the walk out, they chatted freely about their individual lives;

Carrie told him about her second grade school students back in Kentucky and how much she loved seeing their little eyes light up when they learned something new. She explained how she wished she'd come back to Tennessee sooner but had let her life in the city take over. Somewhere along the way, she'd forgotten how special it was here.

Neil shared about his family—telling her about his parents and a younger brother, who also lived in Chicago. He explained that his brother was a C.P.A. in a large accounting firm and seemed to really enjoy his work.

Neil stopped several times to take photos of the wildflowers in the surrounding woods, and even got a few more shots of Carrie. He explained about lighting and what an important part it played in photography. He told her he'd discovered that early mornings and late afternoons were the best time to take his exterior photographs as the angle of the sun gave the photos more depth. Sunlight in the morning tended to give the colors more of a blue tone, whereas dusk gave his photos more of a warm rosy-colored tone. He also told her about how he'd left an extremely well-paying job in Chicago to move here because of the stress of his job and the city. About how he'd felt the Lord had led him here to start a new life doing what he loved.

And how he'd never been sorry.

When they got back to the car it was late enough in the day they decided to head home; but not before they finalized plans to come back to the Cove the next day. He didn't know about Carrie, but he couldn't remember a recent time when he'd enjoyed spending the day with someone as much as he'd delighted in being with her.

He could hardly wait for the next day.

The Healing Hills

CHAPTER 8

Unfortunately, Carrie woke the next morning to the sound of heavy rain pounding on the cabin roof and thunder echoing across the mountains, so she knew even before Neil's apologetic phone call that their second trip to Cades Cove would have to wait for another day. She smiled at the sound of Neil's voice on the other end of the phone, telling her how sorry he was—like he was personally responsible for Tennessee's weather. She didn't know who was more disappointed—him or her.

After Neil's phone call, she decided to be lazy and crawled back into her bed and under the blankets. She closed her eyes for a time and listened to the low rumble of thunder echoing across the mountains.

Finally when she couldn't stand it any longer, she got out of bed to start her day. After she took a quick shower and dressed in a comfortable pair of sweats and an old tee shirt, she ate a bowl of cereal and drank a cup of coffee—then a second one. She washed up her breakfast dishes, then wandered around the cabin and wondered what she was going to do with the rest of the day. She knew she could always make the drive into town to see her aunt at *Meyers Place*—maybe even hang out for the day and find some way to be helpful. But after her emotional breakdown in front of Neil the day before, she really didn't want to be around people today. She felt like she needed to do some emotional healing before she was ready to face a crowd again. And, as she gazed out the window, she wasn't excited about going out into the deluge of rain falling unless she absolutely had to.

Carrie strolled into the bedroom and leisurely straightened up her bed, then scanned the room, looking for anything else that needed tidying. When her eyes fell on the open closet door, she got an idea. The evening Carrie had been to Aunt Myrtle's house for dinner, her aunt had mentioned that she thought there was a small trunk in the back of the closet filled with old family photographs. She had told Carrie she was more than welcome to have copies made of any of them she wanted.

Sounded like a perfect project for a rainy day.

Pushing the hangers holding her clothes aside, Carrie easily found the trunk in the back corner of the closet, and tugged it out so she could carry it into the living room. She sat it down on the low table in front of the couch and sat down in front of it. Carefully pulling the top open, she looked inside and grinned. Aunt Myrtle hadn't been lying when she said there were a lot of old photos. By the looks of things, there were hundreds, if not more, of old family photographs. Some were in photo albums, held on aged heavy paper pages with brittle scotch tape or those small triangle-shaped photo holders Carrie had seen in her parents' old photo albums. Others were stacked loosely in the truck or stuck haphazardly into re-used manila envelopes. As Carrie went through the loose photos, Carrie was astonished to discover a great many of them didn't have any names on the back and wondered how in the world she was ever going to figure out who they all were.

While the rain continued to come down outside and the rumble of thunder eventually faded into the distant mountains, Carrie spent her morning carefully going through the contents of the trunk and sorting the photographs into three stacks—photos of family she recognized, photos with names on them but of people she didn't know, and photos of places and/or people completely unknown to her. The last two batches would have to be taken to Aunt Myrtie, and hopefully she would be able to help Carrie fill in the blanks. Carrie was also counting on her aunt having stories to go with each of the photos she'd found.

A little after noon Carrie finally stopped working on the photos and fixed a hot lunch of canned vegetable beef soup for her lunch, then changed into jeans and a sweatshirt and grabbed her car keys. If she was going to do anything about getting copies of these photos, she needed a scanner. It was a shame really; she had a very expensive scanner/printer at home, but that wasn't going to do her any good here. Hopefully the small office supply store in town would have something that would do the job without causing her to go broke.

The rain had let up some from the early morning's deluge, so Carrie carefully made her way down the mountainside for the drive into town. The store had one model of scanner/printer in stock which was more expensive than what Carrie had hoped, but since she didn't want to make the long drive into Maryville or even farther, she made the decision to go ahead and buy it. She would take it back to Lexington with her in the fall and have it for a spare in case either hers or Ashlynn's quit working.

Once she returned to the cabin, she quickly went to work scanning and documenting into her laptop the family photos of the folks she knew. There were many that brought smiles to her face; photos of her Grandma Violet and Aunt Myrtie when they were little girls, playing on the front porch floor of what looked like a rough-hewn cabin. There were photos of Uncle Jasper as a boy of about ten or so, leading a cow by a rope, an old cow bell hanging around the animal's neck. Carrie was especially excited when she found a really old one of her great-grandfather and great-grandmother Foust and two of their children when they were just babies.

Both of them were dressed in their Sunday best—her great-grandfather wearing a suit, and he didn't look very comfortable in it. Her great-grandmother was dressed in a fancy dark colored dress and a wide-brimmed hat and sat in a wooden straight backed chair in front of a cabin with old Clyde standing behind her. Carrie wondered how often they had worn those clothes as she knew they had been simple farmers who had lived in Cades Cove, and didn't have much in the way of money.

She also found several photos of Uncle Jasper and her Grandpa Bert, who were brothers. Her favorite one was of the two of them at about eight or nine years old, their pant legs rolled up, and fishing poles slung across their shoulders. They looked like Huckleberry Finn and Tom Sawyer. She laughed out loud when she came across that one. It was precious.

When she'd been a little girl, Carrie had been confused by the notion that her Uncle Jasper Meyers and Grandpa Bert Meyers were brothers who had married the two Foust girls, Myrtle and Violet. Now that she was an adult, it still confused her at times to know that Aunt Myrtle's sons were really her double cousins—cousins from both sides of the family. Unfortunately though, they were so much older than she, they had never been close.

Carrie didn't spend a great deal of time looking at the photos as she scanned them into her laptop. She would take time later to touch up the damaged photos, but right now she just wanted to get them saved into her computer and document who was who so she would have copies to take home with her. Then she would have to take the rest of them down to Aunt Myrtle's house and get them identified.

Mysteries to be solved. She loved it.

^^^^^

Neil touched his paintbrush to the canvas in front of him, leaving a small point of lemon yellow hue on the spot. He'd spent hours in his studio working on this particular painting over the past month and after all that time it was finally starting to take shape. After a few more minutes of working, he stood from his perch on a stool in front of the easel, put his brush and palette down on the nearby table and stretched, then walked over to look out the tall wall of windows.

The wind-driven rain still splashed against the glass and the thunder continued to rumble around the skies, bouncing from mountainside to mountainside. He normally loved thunderstorms, but today the sound of the rain and thunder just made him feel lonely. He'd been terribly disappointed that he and Carrie hadn't been able to go back to the Cove today. It surprised him how much he'd enjoyed spending the previous day with her.

He headed across the hall to the main part of his house and made a beeline for the kitchen. It was after two o'clock, and he hadn't had any lunch yet, and he suddenly realized he was hungry. It didn't happen very often, but every now and then he became so involved with a project he was working on, he'd forget to eat. Now his stomach was complaining about the lack of food and he could feel a headache coming on. It was time to listen to his body and feed it. Ten minutes later he sat down at the kitchen table with a ham, cheese and onion omelet the size of his plate. As the steam came up from his food, he bowed his head to thank God for providing for him again, then took up his fork and dug in. It was hot and tasty. Just what he needed to return him to feeling a little more like himself.

While he ate, he allowed his mind to drift to what had been his original plan for the day. He had really been looking forward to spending another day with Miss Myrtle's niece, Carrie Montgomery. When he called to cancel their date and apologize to Carrie, he had almost blurted out how sorry he was that he wasn't going to get to spend another day with her. Fortunately though, he'd stopped before doing so. After knowing each other such a short time, she would have thought he was crazy. And the last thing she needed in her life was another crazy stalker.

The only conciliation he had was that when they talked on the phone that morning, Carrie had sounded almost as sad about not getting to go back to the Cove as he was. He wasn't going to fool himself into believing she was disappointed about not spending the day with him again though.

It had been a long time since he had enjoyed himself like that—just him and a beautiful young woman. While he thought about the talk they'd had at the Falls, his mind returned to Carrie's divulging the specifics about her attack. No wonder she had a constant look of fear about her. After all she had been through, it wasn't surprising at all.

Even though they had both bared their souls to each other, Neil had been shocked at how easy it had been for him to sit there and talk with her—or just sit quietly with her and not say anything at all. He'd dated a few times after Lisa's death, but had never found anyone he could talk with— anyone he felt like sharing his hopes and dreams with. He hadn't felt that comfortable around a woman since…Lisa. At the thought of his wife, Neil bowed his head and sighed. For a few precious hours yesterday, the pain of losing his wife had disappeared and he had almost felt normal again. He wasn't sure he liked the feeling and the guilt that surrounded it.

He strolled across the room to a small table and picked up a framed photo. It was the final photo he had of Lisa and Kaylee—taken their last Christmas together. Lisa and Kaylee had been sitting on the floor in front of their Christmas tree, both of them grinning up at him as he shot the photograph. They had been so happy that day—with no idea of what the future held for them and how little time they had left together.

Even after all these years, he still missed them so much.

Yes, he understood some of the pain Carrie Montgomery was feeling. She'd lost her sense of safety and peace of mind; he'd lost the love of his life and his baby daughter. But at least she had a chance of getting her life back. His former life was gone forever.

∧∧∧∧∧∧

Later in the day a surprise phone call from her roommate, Ashlynn, brought a smile to Carrie's face.

"How ya doing, girl?" her friend's voice sounded as chipper as ever.

Carrie sat back into the cushions of the couch and listened to another clap of thunder in the distance.

"I'd be better if it wasn't storming and pouring right now."

She heard her friend's laugh on the other end of the phone. "Did you have plans to go for a hike in the woods or something?"

Carrie smiled to herself. She was sure Ashlynn was just being flippant, not realizing how on the money she was with her question.

"As a matter of fact," she said slowly, wondering how much she should say to her friend, "I did have plans before this miserable thunderstorm ruined them."

"Oh," Ashlynn replied. "So, you're doing good, then? I've been kinda worried about you."

Worried. Well, Carrie could understand that. She'd been worried about her too when she'd left Lexington to come here.

"I'm really doing pretty good, Ash, considering. I've been sleeping much better—fewer nightmares and I've been getting outside into the beautiful mountains and hills around here and getting some exercise. I think coming here was a good decision."

She heard what sounded like a sigh of relief on the other end of the line. "I'm glad to hear it, Carrie. I still miss you though."

Ashlynn talked for a few moments about end of school year stuff and her plans for the upcoming summer months. She was going to do some traveling to visit her family in Washington State, and also take a couple of weeks to go to London for a trip just before school started again.

Then the topic turned back to Carrie. "So, have you met any good-looking guys down there, Carrie? Or are they all hicks with their dogs and shotguns."

Carrie laughed what to her sounded like a nervous laugh and hoped her roommate didn't pick up on it. No such luck as there was a moment of silence, then her friend's response.

"You have met someone, haven't you?" She heard a little squeal on the other end of the phone and grimaced at the sound. Ashlynn wouldn't let go now, but would continue to badger her with questions.

"I did meet a nice man, Ashlynn. He has an art gallery/store in town. Aunt Myrtle is friends with him and he seems very nice." Carrie stopped, not wanting to divulge any more information than she had to.

"So," her friend prodded. "Is he handsome? Is he old, or young, or just right?"

Carrie couldn't help but laugh at her roommate's exuberance for the topic once she got started. Ashlynn was between boyfriends right now, but had a romantic side of her that would rival the Hallmark Channel.

"I guess you could say he'd good-looking and no, he's not old." She released a sad sigh before she realized she'd done it. "We're just friends though."

Ashlynn picked up on the sigh and the hesitation. "But you're thinking you might want to be more than friends with him, aren't you?"

Carrie stared out the rain splattered window and wondered how to answer her friend's question. "I don't know, Ash. After all I've been through, the last thing I need is another bad relationship. And he's been through some rough times too—lost his wife and little girl in a car accident several years ago—and I'm not sure he's over it yet. I sure don't need to get involved with someone who has more ghosts than I do. And anyway, I just met the man."

"Just don't be afraid to open yourself up to another man, Carrie. Just because Sean's a jerk doesn't mean they all are, you know?"

She nodded, and then agreed verbally with her friend. After a few more minutes talking about how Ashlynn was doing, they said their good-byes and Carrie disconnected the call. It was good to talk with her friend, but hearing her voice brought back memories of what things had been like before the night when her entire life changed.

∧∧∧∧∧

After Ashlynn's phone call, Carrie spent another hour scanning two more stacks of photos into her laptop. She was just thinking about stopping for a while when her cell phone rang again. She grabbed it from the table in front of her and smiled when she saw the caller ID.

"Hi, Aunt Myrtie. What's happening?"

She heard her aunt laugh on the other side. "Can't surprise you, can I. I'm not sure I like all these new-fangled phones where it tells you who's calling before you even answer it."

Carrie grinned. "Sorry, Aunt Myrtle. No surprising me."

There was another chuckle on the other end of the phone. "Anyway, I called to find out if you wanted go to church with me in the morning." Carrie heard what sounded like several people talking in the background and dishes banging.

"Are you at the restaurant?"

She heard her aunt cover the phone with her hand while she talked to someone else briefly, then she was back. "Yes. Charlie needed the afternoon off, so he came in this morning and I took the afternoon/evening shift." Carrie heard the sound of the cash register opening, then heard her aunt thank a customer.

"Anyway, I usually go to church early so I can go to Sunday school, but since I'll be here late tonight, I won't go until the regular worship service and I thought you might want to go with me. You could stop and pick me up, and we could go together...."

Carrie felt like groaning. It was obvious her aunt was encouraging her to start attending church again. Somewhere in one of their talks, she must have mentioned she hadn't been going as regularly as she used to.

"I guess I can do that," she finally answered. No sleeping in tomorrow morning, but then she really didn't need to. She'd been lazy for the past week and maybe it would do her good to get out around people again. She just wasn't looking forward to all the questions.

"Oh good!" her aunt said. "And I'll have a roast in the oven when we get out of church, so you can plan on eating with me. How's that sound?"

Carrie laughed. "It sounds great, Aunt Myrtie. Are you fixing it with those little potatoes and carrots and onions like you used to?"

"Of course," she heard on the other end of the call.

Her aunt told her what time to pick her up and ended the call, telling Carrie she had to get off the phone as a large group of folks had just come into the restaurant.

After ending the call, Carrie felt a moment of guilt for not being at the restaurant to help. Sure, her aunt had other employees, but Carrie felt after everything her aunt had done for her over the years, she needed to do more for her. Maybe next week she'd spend some time at the restaurant. Hopefully there was something she could do to help Aunt Myrtle out. She'd never worked as a waitress, but if necessary, she could always wash dishes or bus tables.

Carrie finished scanning in the last stack of photos, then got up from the table and fixed herself some dinner. Tonight was going to be an early night, and hopefully because it was a cooler evening with a light rain still falling outside, it would be good sleeping weather.

Her last thought as she tried to go to sleep was wondering where Neil Johnston went to church.

The Healing Hills

CHAPTER 9

The next morning, Carrie groaned when she woke to the sound of her alarm. She hadn't been setting the alarm since she'd come to the mountains, but hadn't wanted to oversleep this morning. She reached over to shut off the annoying sound, then stretched and yawned. She'd promised her aunt she would take her to church, so it was time get up and start the day.

An hour later she stood in front of the full length mirror on the back of the bedroom door, studying her reflection. Did the gray skirt and red blouse she was wearing make her look too matronly? She wanted to look serious enough to go to church, but she didn't want to look like an old lady. She'd already tried on two dresses and rejected both of them as being either too fancy or too summer-ish. Like it or not, the skirt and blouse would have to do.

The next problem was what to do with her hair. Her blond hair, a little longer than shoulder-length, was due for a trim, and recently she had been either pulling it back in a ponytail, or braiding it. Running her hairbrush through it another time, she decided this morning she would just wear it down around her shoulders.

Slipping her feet into her black pumps, she grabbed her purse and keys and threw the lock on the door on her way out. Before her feet got to the first step though, she paused, then turned back and unlocked the door and went back into the cabin. If she was going to church, she needed a Bible to take with her. She grabbed her great-grandfather's old Bible off the table next to the couch, and then repeated her exit again. Hopefully Aunt Myrtle wouldn't have a problem with her using the old book. Carrie would just be very careful with it. Too bad she hadn't thought to bring her own Bible. Of course, she wasn't even sure where it was, but had to assume it was stuck in a drawer someplace back in her apartment.

Aunt Myrtle was already coming down the back steps when Carrie pulled her car into the drive next to the house, the sound of her aunt scolding Buster for wanting to brush up against her dress coming through Carrie's open car window.

"Buster, get down before you get doggy hair all over me. Good mornin', darling," her aunt sang out with a smile as she opened the passenger door and got in the car.

"Good morning, Aunt Myrtle. How are you doing this morning?"

She heard her aunt's sigh. "Feeling rather weary, but I guess that's not surprising after working the late shift yesterday. Guess I'm getting old."

Carrie glanced across the car in concern and studied her aunt's face for a moment. She noticed the tired lines around the older woman's eyes and wondered if it might be time for the older woman to think seriously about selling the restaurant and retiring. She couldn't keep up the long hours forever. But Carrie knew enough about her aunt to know that right now on the way to church wasn't the time to bring up the topic.

The rest of the fifteen minute drive through the mountains on the narrow twisty roads was relatively silent as Carrie concentrated on keeping track of where they were going. She hadn't been to the little country church in years, but was fairly certain she knew how to get there. It was good to see the white framed steeple in the distance though as she turned the final curve.

She found a spot in the gravel parking lot to park her car before she and her aunt exited the car and headed across the lot to the church. Carrie glanced around, noticing how many cars were here. It had been a long time since she'd been here—the summer she was thirteen. But between Vacation Bible Schools and Sunday school classes, she'd spent almost as many hours in this church during her childhood summers as she had her parents' church back in Knoxville.

As soon as they entered through the wide oak double doors of the old church, Aunt Myrtle was greeted by numerous friends and Carrie found herself being introduced to everyone around them. An older gentleman acting as an usher handed her a bulletin, then her Aunt Myrtle grabbed hold of her arm and led her to what Carrie remembered as the pew she and Uncle Jasper had always sat it; sixth pew on the left hand side—about half-way up. As the old polished oak floors creaked under their feet, Carrie felt herself relax. Everything was just as she remembered, and again she had the feeling of coming home. It made her feel good to know some things in life remained the same.

As they took their seats in the pews though, Carrie couldn't help but notice there were a few changes in the church building around her. The front now sported a new smaller podium with a more modern microphone, and the old organ had been replaced with a baby grand piano. Carrie also noticed the area where the choir had always sat now sat empty. The days of having a choir in a church seemed to have disappeared, along with so many other things from the past.

Carrie looked through the bulletin as she sat quietly in the pew, trying not to pay attention to the feeling that all eyes in the church were trained on her and Aunt Myrtie. Then she reminded herself it was only because this was her first Sunday here. She would only have to undergo this for a Sunday or two. In a few weeks, she would just be another face in the congregation and they would be accustomed to having her here again. She knew it was only because they cared. In a small town, people were more connected than back in the city.

The pastor, who Aunt Myrtle had introduced to her as Pastor Gregory, had just appeared behind the podium and asked them to stand for the first song when Carrie felt someone slide into the pew next to her. She turned and was shocked to look into the face of Neil Johnston.

"Good morning," he whispered. "I hope it's okay if I sit with you and Myrtle."

She smiled back at him, suddenly feeling like the day had brightened a little bit. "Of course," she whispered back, then handed him her open hymnal which she'd already turned to the first song. When she made a move to get another hymnal to use, he shook his head and held out the hymnal so she could hold onto half of it.

The rest of the morning was a blur as Carrie struggled with the knowledge that a very handsome man was sitting right next to her. She tried to concentrate on the sermon, which she was certain was very good, but all she could do was wonder why Neil Johnston had chosen to come to church this morning and sit next to her. Then again, maybe this was the church he normally attended. Maybe he always sat next to Aunt Myrtle. She'd never asked and he'd never told her. But he could have chosen to sit anywhere, next to anyone. Why had he decided to sit next to her? Was he just trying to make her feel welcome by being a supporting friend? Or was he doing it for Aunt Myrtle? Or was he feeling the same attraction between the two of them that she was starting to feel? An attraction that was terrifying to her.

By the end of the sermon and the beginning of the closing song, she had scolded herself countless times, telling herself it didn't mean anything and was only because of his association with Aunt Myrtie that he was sitting next to her. He was just being friendly.

It didn't matter anyway. She didn't want to get involved with a man right now, after all. Wasn't that what she had decided?

∧∧∧∧∧∧

Neil knew he had confused Carrie by showing up at church and sitting next to her. He normally sat by himself near the back, but this morning he had felt drawn to sit with her and her aunt. After he did so, he started to feel like every eye in the church was burning into his back and he wondered if he'd made a wise decision. The older church ladies' tongues would surely wag now. He could almost hear the chatter that would be spreading around after the service:

That Neil Johnston must have his sights on Myrtle Meyers' grand-niece. Did you see them sitting together this morning in church? They do make a nice-lookin' couple though.

Well, there wasn't anything he could do about it now, and in the meantime he was here and was going to enjoy the opportunity to have someone to sit with during the service. He'd spent way too many Sundays sitting by himself.

Carrie didn't even appear to remember he was sitting next to her most of the time; her eyes were glued to the pastor at the front of the church or turned down to follow some scripture in the well-worn Bible in her lap. He kept wondering if it was her Bible. If so, she was sure to be more knowledgeable about the Bible than he would be; although since his family's death, he'd taken to reading it more and more—needing the comfort and wisdom between the covers.

He'd learned he couldn't survive without the presence of God in his life.

Neil tried his best to concentrate on the sermon, but found his mind wandering time and time again to the discussions he and Carrie had back at Abrams Falls. He also spent some time trying to decipher the attraction he felt for her. Somewhere along the way, Carrie Montgomery had broken down his barriers of the last four years and touched his heart in ways he forgot. He hadn't felt this type of fascination with a woman since he met Lisa.

It alarmed him. He wasn't sure he was ready for these feelings rushing through him. Being friends with Carrie Montgomery was one thing. Wanting to pull her into his arms and kiss her was another thing.

So, after church he greeted both Carrie and her aunt, and politely declined Miss Myrtle's offer of Sunday lunch, deciding instead to go home and do some soul-searching. He had originally planned to ask Carrie to go to the Cove again with him sometime in the near future, but after the feelings he'd just had rush over him while he sat next to her on the pew, he decided instead to back away from spending any more time with her right now. They hadn't known each other long and even though she seemed like a very nice woman, and even though she was Myrtle's niece, he needed to have some time to think things through a little better. If he were this attracted to her already, where would it lead if he were to spend more time with her?

The better question was, what would happen in a couple of months when her summer vacation was over and she returned to her teaching job and life in the city? Where would that leave him?

No, it was best this way. He didn't want to set his heart up for any more sadness than what he'd already suffered.

Carrie was surprised how disappointed she felt when she heard Neil politely decline Aunt Myrtle's offer of lunch, even though another part of her was relieved. She had felt more than a little nervous this morning while sitting next to him in church, and she couldn't figure out why. Maybe it was because she knew how much of her heart she had bared to this man about what she had been through, or maybe it was because she was frightened of the feelings he stirred up in her. Perhaps it was because of all he had told her about the death of his wife and little girl. It had been obvious by the pain in his voice that he had been very much in love with his wife. It sounded like he wasn't totally over losing her and their little girl, so maybe it was better if Carrie didn't get too friendly with him. Even though Carrie could understand his feelings after having been through her own tragedy, she didn't need to share anyone else's pain.

You never really got over something like that. What was it her therapist had told her? 'The pain of trauma cuts deeply into your soul and often leaves lifetime scars.'

She had enough wounds of her own to heal. She certainly didn't need to get caught up in Neil Johnston's agony.

Either way, it appeared she didn't have to worry about it today, and let out a sigh of relief as she and Aunt Myrtle pulled out of the parking lot in Carrie's car and headed home. Her aunt chatted about different friends of hers from church, shared her thoughts about the sermon topic and the songs they had sung, then started talking about her plans for lunch. By the time they'd pulled in the driveway and parked the car next to the house, Carrie's stomach was growling in anticipation of her aunt's beef roast.

During the meal, Aunt Myrtle finally broached the subject of Carrie's attack. Carrie hesitantly shared a few of the basic facts about it, not wanting to upset her elderly aunt any more than necessary.

"Well," Aunt Myrtle said as they finished their dessert, "I'm terribly sorry something like that happened to you, sweetie. But I certainly am glad God brought you back home."

Carrie frowned. She didn't want to insult her aunt, but she was afraid her thoughts on God didn't match hers. "Aunt Myrtie, if God cared so much about me, why didn't he stop Lloyd Taylor from attacking me? I find it hard to believe God loves me when he allowed something like that to happen to me."

The older woman sat silently for a moment, her head bowed. Carrie felt a lump in her throat at the thought that her words had hurt her aunt. She hadn't meant to insult her; she was just being honest. How could a loving God allow all the evil in the world?

Finally Aunt Myrtle spoke. "Let's look at this way, Carolyn: If you hadn't been attacked—if it hadn't happened to you—would you have come back here? Maybe this whole incident was to draw you back here to the mountains—and back to your faith in God."

Carrie didn't have an answer for that, so remained silent as her Aunt Myrtle stood and walked over and gave her a quick hug, then together they washed and dried the dirty dishes.

Later after the kitchen was spotless, Carrie went out and grabbed the box of photos from the back seat of her car and brought them into the house. The rest of the afternoon, the two of them pored over the photo albums and loose pictures Carrie had found in the cabin. While Aunt Myrtle looked at the faded faces of people long gone, she shared tales about Carrie's grandmother's and her own childhood—most of them stories Carrie had never heard. Not trusting her memory, she scribbled everything in her notepad as fast as she could. The more her aunt talked, the more excited Carrie became. There were some real stories here—not just about the Meyers and Foust families—but also about the people and customs of the mountains—tales about a way of life that had vanished.

Aunt Myrtle also shared some of the old stories of folklore she had grown up with. Carrie's pen sped over the notepad as she tried to write them down. Carrie's favorite was a tall tale about a man who lived on the side of a mountain so steep, that when it came time to harvest his apple trees, he only had to shake the trees and the apples would roll down the side of the mountain and into the bushel baskets he had laid out near his back porch. Carrie tried to get the story down on paper the way her Aunt Myrtle told it, but it was impossible to include the facial expressions and motions that could only be seen when hearing the story in person. Aunt Myrtle told her that very tale had been told her countless times by her grandfather Foust when she was just a wee little girl and had been passed down generation to generation by the dwellers of the Smokies.

Before Carrie realized it, she glanced down at her wristwatch and was shocked to discover it was almost six o'clock in the evening. The whole afternoon had flown by.

"I'm sorry, Aunt Myrtle. I should have let you rest this afternoon. I didn't intend to take up your whole day."

Her aunt waved her hand at her as if in dismissal. "Are you kidding? I've had a grand old time going through these photos with you." She smiled and patted Carrie on the arm. "I wish my own boys and grandkids would get this excited about their ancestors. It does my heart good to see you so interested in all the old stories and photos."

She waved her hands in the direction on the boxes of photos. "Do you know what you're gonna do with all this?"

Carrie shook her head. "I'm not sure yet. I originally planned on just doing a scrapbook sort of thing for the family—you know, kind of a family history. But you have so many stories about other people and old neighbors of yours—maybe I could even get something published eventually. I don't know...we'll see."

Her aunt nodded her approval. "I bet there are city folks who would be interested in reading about how mountain life used to be." Her eyes lit up. "You could probably sell some of those books in shops around the Smokies or maybe even in the Cades Coves gift shop."

Carrie's mind raced with the possibility, but she just smiled at her aunt's enthusiasm. "Well, I don't know about that. I'm hardly a writer."

Aunt Myrtle pulled out leftovers for some sandwiches, and after the two of them had eaten and Carrie had helped to clean up the kitchen again, she headed up the mountain to the cabin. It had been a long busy day, but she was so thankful she'd been able to spend it with her aunt.

And the time spent with Neil Johnston hadn't been all that bad either.

CHAPTER 10

Monday morning, Carrie was up early and eating breakfast when her cell phone rang. She smiled when she saw the name listed on the caller ID and quickly answered it.

"Good morning, Mom."

"Good morning, yourself." She could almost envision her mother smiling as she heard her voice through the phone.

"Haven't heard from you and wanted to make sure you arrived all right and that you're doing okay. I had hoped you'd give us a call when you got there...."

Carrie chided herself for not having thought to call her parents when she first arrived. "I'm so sorry, Mom. I just got so busy going places and doing things with Aunt Myrtle, I forgot to call you."

She paused for breath. "But, I'm doing okay, really. I'm trying to keep busy so I don't have too much time to think about it all, you know?"

She heard her mother's deep sigh on the other end of the phone. "Yes, dear. And doing some fun things will be good for you, but if you need us for anything, please call. I've been very worried about you. Have you been to see your new psychologist yet?"

Carrie bit her lower lip to try and stop the tears she could feel building up in her eyes. It helped to know her parents still loved her and worried about her, but she was a grown adult and it wasn't their job to make everything perfect for her. She had to work through this mental/emotional problem by herself.

"I have an appointment to go see her today, Mom. But, really. I'm doing okay. Please don't worry about me." She took her dirty dishes over to the sink and ran water on them while still trying to keep hold of her phone. "I'll have to call you back later, though as I'm kind of in a hurry. I was just getting ready for my appointment."

"Okay, dear. Please give Aunt Myrtle our love, and Carolyn," her mom cleared her throat and Carrie closed her eyes at the sound of her real name. "Dad and I love you so very much, and so does God. Just remember that, okay? You're not going through this alone." There was a pause for a few seconds before her mom added, "Oh, and I hope you're planning on spending a couple days with us before you head back to Kentucky in the fall."

Carrie sighed. Her mom's faith that God was still in control always made her feel unsettled, but she wasn't going to say anything over the phone. Not when she needed to get going.

"Yes, Mom. I'm planning to visit you and Dad before I go home, and I'll call you in a few days so we can talk more, okay? But, I really need to go now."

She finally ended the call, feeling guilty at being relieved it was over. She knew she really should have contacted her parents when she'd first arrived, but hadn't done it for that exact reason. She didn't want to be reminded of how much they too had been affected by the attack on her. Her dad had been crushed to think something like that had happened to his little girl and he hadn't been there to protect her..

Carrie had dressed casually that morning in jeans with a little dressier than she normally would have worn, but because she had this appointment with the therapist she wanted to look nice. Instead of braiding her hair or pulling it back in to a ponytail, she'd just brushed it out until it shone and left it hanging down around her shoulders. She couldn't believe how much it had grown.

After finishing a few more things at the cabin, she left to make the drive into town. Following the directions to Dr. Martin's office she had printed from the internet, she easily found the office in the older downtown area of Maryville. Even though it was an old brick building on the outside, inside it was a pleasantly decorated building with a small office in the front for a receptionist, and Dr. Martin's office in the rear. As she followed the receptionist back to the doctor's office, she tried unsuccessfully to calm her nerves. This wasn't the first time she'd met with a psychologist; surely she could handle having to go through the experience again.

Carrie was pleasantly surprised to find Dr. Susan Martin was a woman in her early thirties, not much older than Carrie. Dr. Martin got up from her desk to greet her shortly after she came through the door, her hand already outstretched to shake Carrie's.

"I'm happy to meet you, Carrie. Please have a seat so we can chat a bit."

Carrie sat down while Dr. Martin asked her questions about the information in the file that had been forwarded to her by the school psychologist. Dr. Martin quickly told her to call her Susan, and assured her that in this meeting they weren't going to do anything more than talk. When Carrie was ready to discuss what had happened to her, then they would talk about it.

An hour later she was feeling a little more comfortable with meeting Susan once a week for the remainder of the summer. Before she left the office, Susan assured her she would do everything she could to help Carrie get to where she was ready to return to her teaching job and classroom in the fall.

Carrie prayed that would be the case.

∧∧∧∧∧

Later that afternoon, Carrie went to the restaurant to help her aunt. She had promised to do so, and after the brief talk with her therapist that morning, she felt mentally ready to take on a new challenge. She'd sat around feeling sorry for herself long enough.

When she walked through the front door of the restaurant, Aunt Myrtle seemed surprised to see her at first, but then quickly put her busy bussing tables, washing dishes in the kitchen, and training her on ringing up sales. The rest of the day flew by and before Carrie knew it, it was time for her to go home.

After a few days had passed working at the restaurant, Carrie was starting to understand how things worked and was even waiting on tables and taking orders, along with pouring coffee for the customers. Sadie and Kathy, the two college-aged waitresses, welcomed her into their midst, and in only a day or two were kidding and joking with her and treating her as if she were one of them. It gave Carrie a sense of well-being to know she was finally helping the loving aunt who had done so much for her over the years. Carrie also enjoyed spending the time with the younger girls who made her feel at home—even when she dropped a stack of dirty dishes on the kitchen floor with a tremendous crash.

Aunt Myrtle quickly made it understood to her, however, that if she was going to work there, she was going to be paid. Even though Carrie objected and tried to insist she didn't want to be paid, Aunt Myrtle wasn't going to have any of it.

"But I'm already staying in the cabin for free, Aunt Myrtle. You don't need to pay me."

Her aunt shook her head firmly. "Don't argue with me, young lady."

Carrie sighed in defeat. She remembered that tone of voice from past summers. When Aunt Myrtle got an idea in her head, there wasn't any use arguing with her.

Once Carrie began working at the restaurant, the next two weeks passed quickly. She felt like her weekly sessions with Susan were also going well. Maybe it was because she had already shared the story with Neil, but when it came time to tell the therapist about the attack, Carrie was able to do so without breaking down. Susan asked her some different questions than her other therapist had asked, especially how Carrie felt about what the attack had done to her—both physically and mentally. She had come highly recommended as a Christian psychologist, and Carrie felt very comfortable around her. Susan talked with her about much more than just the attack though, and Carrie started to feel like she was more of a friend than a therapist. Somewhere along the way, she had even shared her new friendship with Neil Johnston and how much of a comfort it had been to talk to him about the attack.

The only time Carrie saw Neil was when he would occasionally stop in the restaurant for lunch. He still sat next to her and her aunt every Sunday at church, was always very friendly, but never suggested making another trip to Cades Cove with him. Part of her was disappointed he hadn't invited her on another outing, although she comforted herself with the knowledge that he was probably just busy now that the summer tourist season was in full swing.

The other part of her knew it was best that she didn't spend more time with him. In a couple of months she'd be heading back to Lexington, so there was no sense heading down a road that would only lead to heartache.

∧∧∧∧∧

One day in late May, right after Memorial Day, Carrie received a phone call from Karla Stanfield, the District Attorney in Lexington. When she saw the caller ID, her heart lurched. She hadn't heard from the DA's office in months and couldn't think of any reason why they'd be contacting her now.

"Hi, Carrie. How's it going?" Carrie smiled a little at the upbeat voice of the thirty-something career woman on the other end of the phone. DA Stanfield was a petite woman with a dynamo personality, and had battled hard to see to it Carrie received justice for what had been done to her during the attack.

"I'm fine, Ms. Stanfield, I guess...." She let her words trail off, wondering if this was a good-news call or a bad-news call. "What's up?"

"Well," the other woman stated. "I just wanted to let you know what's going on. I received a phone call from Matthew Jennings."

Carrie heart lurched again. Matthew Jennings was the man who had acted as Defense Attorney for Lloyd Taylor, the man who had attacked her. Why would he have called the DA?

She felt her heart rate double and took a big breath as she tried to get air into her lungs.

"I don't know for sure what it's about yet, but wanted to let you know Jennings has requested a meeting in Judge Stapleton's chambers," Karla quickly said.

Making her way across the cabin, Carrie sunk into the soft cushions of the couch. Her legs suddenly felt weak and she didn't want to be standing to hear the rest of this.

"Why?" was all she could finally squeak out, feeling as if Lloyd Taylor was strangling her all over again.

"I'm guessing it might be about an appeal, but I won't know for sure until our meeting." Ms. Stanfield's voice became a little firmer. "I'm sorry, Carrie. I was hoping they wouldn't pursue an appeal."

Carrie shook her head in disbelief as the familiar feeling of terror ran over her. Just when she thought she was safe—just when she was starting to feel a little more normal—now this. Why? Why would God let this happen?

The other woman's voice brought her back to the conversation. "The meeting is in a couple of weeks. I'll let you know what's happening as soon as I can. In the meantime, try not to worry about it too much. Taylor is in prison and can't hurt you anymore, and chances of him winning an appeal are slim to none."

Carrie dropped her head in sorrow. Easy for the DA to say. She wasn't the one whose life would never be the same.

CHAPTER 11

The next two weeks returned Carrie mentally to the point she had been right after the trial. Once again she had trouble sleeping, being haunted with the familiar nightmares and night terrors. She knew if Lloyd Taylor won the right to appeal his case, she'd more than likely have to go back and testify again. And what would she do if he was found not-guilty this time? He'd be set free, and she couldn't live with the knowledge that he could come back and hurt her again.

Suddenly the sessions with Dr. Martin weren't helping much—mostly because Carrie felt as if she was living with a ticking time bomb. It felt good to be able to share her fears with Dr. Martin, but there wasn't much the other woman could say to make her feel any better about the situation. Not knowing what was going to happen was almost more than Carrie could stand.

She kept recalling Dr. Martin's words to her during their last session: "You're safe, not because of the absence of danger in your life, Carrie; but because of the presence of God. He's with you—always."

If only those words offered her the peace she so desperately craved.

The only time she didn't feel stressed out about the whole situation was when she was at the restaurant, working with her Aunt Myrtle and the others. Schools were out now, and the tourists had arrived in the mountains in full force, so the restaurant was buzzing with new business.

The evening right after the phone call from the DA, Carrie had gone to see her aunt, needing the comfort of the older woman's loving arms as she sobbed out her fears.

"I can't believe this is happening, Aunt Myrtle," she cried. "Why is God letting this happen? I don't understand."

Her aunt hadn't said much of anything that evening. Instead she had simply held her and let her cry. It was probably just as well at that point. Carrie wasn't in the mood to hear any platitudes about how much God loved her.

A few days later though, when Carrie's emotions weren't quite so fragile, Aunt Myrtle invited her to the old farmhouse for dinner. The words Carrie had dreaded hearing were finally spoken.

"God still loves you, girl. Nothing's changed there."

Carrie simply shook her head. She sure didn't feel loved.

"How can anything good come from this, Aunt Myrtle?"

Aunt Myrtle took Carrie's hands in hers and looked straight in her eyes. "I firmly believe God is working on this situation right now, Carolyn. Don't you give up your faith in His ability to turn this around for your good."

∧∧∧∧∧∧

The end of the next week, Carrie was at the restaurant when she received the dreaded phone call from the District Attorney.

"Is it a good time to talk, Carrie?" the other woman asked. Carrie ducked through the kitchen and out the back door into the sun-lit alleyway behind the restaurant.

"It's as good a time as any, Karla." She took a deep breath. "So, tell me what happened while I can still bear hearing it."

She heard a little chuckle on the other end of the phone and wanted to snap back at the other woman. How in the world could the District Attorney think this was a laughing matter? Carrie had felt like a basket case ever since the DA's earlier call.

"Relax, Carrie. The meeting was not to request an appeal. Quite the contrary, actually."

Carrie frowned as she looked across the back alleyway toward the direction of the nearest mountain range. What did that mean?

"No appeal?" she finally squeaked out.

"No appeal," Karla repeated.

Carrie heard the other woman take a deep breath on the other end of the phone call before she continued.

"Lloyd Taylor wanted his attorney to pass a message along to the court and to you. He's now admitting his guilt and has stated he does not want an appeal—not now, not ever. According his attorney, Matthew Jennings, Taylor intends to serve every day of his sentence."

Carrie swallowed hard as she tried to comprehend what the other woman was telling her. "I don't understand. Why is he doing this?" Carrie switched her phone to her other ear, wanting to make sure she could hear the DA's answer clearly. Sometimes the cell reception up in the mountains wasn't the best.

"I talked with him in person, Carrie. After the meeting with the judge, we—his attorney, myself, and him—we spent over an hour discussing the case and the outcome. Mr. Taylor sounds like he is truly sorry for what he did to you, and I think in order to prove it, he wants to take his punishment—the entire sentence." Carrie heard a noise through the phone like a shuffling of paperwork. "He wrote you a letter, Carrie, and he would like me to send it to you."

Carrie's head starting shaking negatively even though there was no way the other woman could see it. And she was thankful the DA couldn't see the affect her words were having on her. The hand holding the phone was shaking, and she was so wound up she felt nauseous.

"Karla, please, I can't deal with this right now."

"I know, it's a lot for him or anyone to ask after what you've been through, Carrie. But I do believe he's truly sincere. I've read the letter," Carrie heard the noise again. "As a matter of fact, I have it right here in my hand. There isn't anything here that should be upsetting to you. It's simply to tell you how sorry he is for what he did. He's not even asking you to forgive him."

A fury Carrie had never experienced swept over her. "Forgive him? How dare he think all he has to do is say he's sorry? He destroyed my life!"

"He's not asking for forgiveness, Carrie," The District Attorney's voice had turned soft as if she were trying to sooth Carrie over the phone. "In reality, you don't have to do anything about this letter, Carrie. He just wants you to have it. You don't even have to read it if you don't want to. There is no way he will ever know one way or the other."

There was a pause for a second or two on the other end of the phone. "But I do have to tell you, Carrie; I've talked to the prison doctor and psychologist about him, and I've also discussed him with the prison chaplain. Since he's been on this new medication, he's made some significant changes in his life. The chaplain says he's totally surrendered his life to God and has become very religious. He's even been leading a Bible study within the prison population for the last three months and has gained the respect of the guards and his fellow inmates. They all believe he's a changed man."

Carrie closed her eyes and dropped her head as she listened to the D.A. tell about how much the man who had destroyed her life had changed. Well he'd changed her life too—and not in a good way. How could Karla think she'd be able to ever forgive him?

"Carrie," the older woman's voice quieted again on the other end of the phone and Carrie had to strain to hear her. "He's not asking for you to respond to his letter or even acknowledge it. Like I said before, you don't even have to read it if you decide you don't want to."

She sighed, her head feeling like it had for weeks after the attack. The discomfort of it pounding made it hard to think, and even more difficult to decide what to do. Here she was, trying her best to put it all behind her, and now this was happening. How was she supposed to go on with her life and forget the terror of that night when things like this kept bringing it all to the forefront of her mind again? Why was God allowing this to happen? Why now?

"Go ahead and mail the letter to me, Karla," she finally said into the phone, feeling defeat sweep over her. "I can't promise I'll ever read it. If I'm smart, I'll just burn the stupid thing without even opening it. But if you send it to me, at least you can tell his attorney you did what you were asked to do."

She heard a sigh of relief on the other end of the phone. "Thank you, Carrie. And for the record, I'd hate to have you burn it without even reading it. I do believe he's being sincere. Like I said before—just hang on to it, and maybe someday you'll be ready to read it."

Carrie closed her eyes and sighed again. The way she felt today, she wasn't sure she would ever get to the point where she was ready.

∧∧∧∧∧∧

In the midst of all the stress, there were a few bright spots in her days.

One evening she received a surprising phone call from Neil Johnston, asking her if she'd like to go to the Cades Cove Museum in Maryville with him. Before she even thought about it, she agreed. It sounded like a place she'd really like to see and after all she'd been through the last two weeks, she was in need of some entertainment. She'd done nothing but work lately, and it was time for a change. She ignored the little voice that kept telling her she was a fool for spending time with a man who made her heart beat a little faster when he was in the same room with her. It was obvious he just wanted to be friends, so she was going to have to carefully guard her heart. Like she'd told her therapist, Susan, when the topic of Neil had come up during one of their sessions; Carrie wasn't willing to try and compete with the ghost of his wife. Until he decided they were capable of being more than just friends, that's all they were going to be.

Neil picked her up the next Saturday morning, and together they made the short drive to Maryville. The Museum, located in the Thompson/Brown House, was a free-of-charge museum and was stuffed full of artifacts and belongings of former residents of the Cove—donated by their families in order to preserve the stories of these hardy people. Carrie was excited to find a wood stove which had been in the Missionary Baptist Church back when it was still being used, antique clocks, a spinning wheel, framed photos of pioneers who had long since passed, and even the last cook stove used in the Cove. Every item had a story to tell, and Carrie and Neil took their time going through the old building, soaking up all the history of the local area. Carrie pulled a small pad of paper from her purse and scribbled down notes about several of the items to include in her family history book. Some of them, she'd never seen before.

All in all it was an enjoyable afternoon, finished with them sharing dinner at a local restaurant famous for their BBQ. They talked about mundane things like the weather and tourist places in the area. It was as if they had both decided not to delve into anything of a personal nature—to keep their distance; but that was fine with Carrie. As long as she got to spend the time with him, she would take it any way she could.

∧∧∧∧∧∧

A week later after the church service, Neil Johnston asked Carrie and her aunt if they would like to accompany him to the upcoming Passion Play which was held during the summer months in a nearby town. Before Carrie could even speak, Aunt Myrtle had answered for both of them.

"Oh, Neil. We'd love to go! I haven't been to the Passion Play in years," Aunt Myrtle expressed her joy. She turned to Carrie, a knowing gleam in her eyes as she smiled at her. "Your Uncle Jasper and I used to go see it every now and then. I don't think you've ever been to it though, have you, dear?"

Carrie shook her head. "No, Aunt Myrtle, I haven't." She sighed in resignation. She looked at Neil and gave him a little smile. "It sounds wonderful, Neil. Thank you for inviting us."

The following Friday night Neil picked them up at Aunt Myrtle's house and drove the short distance into the nearby town where the drama was enacted. When they arrived at their destination, Carrie was surprised by the size of the concrete amphitheater built into the side of the hill with an expansive cement stage below. The place was huge and looked like it would seat several thousand people. Even though they were fairly early, there were already other early arrivals there ahead of them, seated in various spots around them and waiting patiently for the production to begin.

While Neil, Carrie and Aunt Myrtle sat in the amphitheater, Aunt Myrtle shared some of her memories about the place. Carrie listened for a time, but then let her mind drift and turned her head to gaze at the various ranges of the Great Smoky Mountains that ringed the amphitheater. It was a warm summer evening, the air soft and still—a perfect evening for viewing an outside performance. She heard the mournful call of a mourning dove somewhere in the near distance, and then the answering call from another one farther away. As she allowed the stillness of the evening to engulf her, Carrie took a deep breath and felt her weary body relax. Aunt Myrtle had been right. The play hadn't even begun and she was already feeling a long sought for peacefulness fall over her.

As the darkness of the evening approached, Carrie continued to gaze out at the greenish-blue mountains, her eyes drawn to the varying hues of the lush greens of the trees silhouetted against the darkening sky. Carrie continued to watch as the light faded from the sky and the hills melted into the darkness. Then she felt Neil gently elbow her as if to draw her attention back to the stage below.

The play was about to begin.

∧∧∧∧∧

Neil watched Carrie's face as she stared out at the view of the darkening mountains around them. When he'd mentioned the play, he'd been shocked that her aunt and uncle had never brought Carrie to the play when she'd visited the area as a child. He'd decided right then he was going to remedy that. No one should miss out on this wonderful experience.

As evening fell and the play was about to begin, he gently nudged Carrie with his elbow and gave her a little nod, drawing her attention to the stage below. It was about to begin.

Even though he'd seen the play before—which began with Jesus' entry into Jerusalem, moved through the Last Supper and into the betrayal and arrest of Jesus, led to the garden of Gethsemane, and was followed by Jesus' trial before Pilate, his crucifixion, burial and resurrection—Neil was transfixed as the drama unfolded. The music and actors were so good, and he was quickly drawn into the drama until it felt like he was less of a spectator and more of a participant. It was a very moving experience, and when the final line was given sharing the hope and joy of the message of the Resurrection, he was sure the rest of the people in the audience were experiencing the same thing he was; his heart was filled with the ringing notes of triumph over death and sin.

He just hoped Carrie had enjoyed the drama as much as he had.

∧∧∧∧∧∧

As the three of them made their way down the steps from their seats and headed toward Neil's Jeep in the parking lot, it was silent between them. Carrie felt like she had a lot to think about after experiencing the reality of what Jesus had lived through on the cross for her. As Neil drove his Jeep down the darkened country roads to take them back to the farm, she sat quietly in the back seat and prayed.

Heavenly Father, I'm so sorry I've ignored you recently. I'm sorry I blamed you for everything I went through instead of leaning on You like I should have. Lord, I've never really valued all you did for us on the cross that day—the pain and humiliation you experienced at my expense. Please forgive me for how I've turned from Your truth and forgive me for my lack of appreciation. You gave up so much for me. Please help me to be willing to live for you and do what you would desire of me. Thank Your for Your continuing forgiveness.

Later that night while she was in her bed, replaying the evening, Carrie was once again thankful for her decision to come to the mountains. In hindsight, she could see where God had been working on her ever since the first day she had arrived here, and now that she knew Lloyd Taylor wasn't going to be able to hurt her again, she could feel the long-awaited healing process had finally begun. She didn't know if she would ever be completely free of the trauma of the attack, but at least she was on the right track, and she had God to thank for that; God—and the peacefulness of the mountains around her.

∧∧∧∧∧∧

Almost a week after the three of them attended the Passion Play, Carrie woke up on a Thursday morning with an extremely sore throat, body aches, and a killer headache. After managing to eat and keep down a piece of dry toast, she dragged into the bathroom and tried to get ready to go to work. Standing in front of the mirror and seeing how bad she looked, she realized if she was as sick as she felt, the last place she needed to be was around other people's food. When she called her Aunt Myrtle, she told Carrie in a firm voice that she was to go back to bed and call if she felt any worse.

Carrie gulped down a couple of aspirin with some water and headed back to bed. A little after noon, the thermometer she found in the bathroom medicine cabinet stated she was running even more of a fever than she had that morning and she knew she was really sick. She felt so bad though, she didn't think she could make the drive to the clinic in town so just stayed in bed, tossing and turning. While the sweaty sheets stuck to her, she kept wondering why everything in the room continued to shift and roll.

She finally dozed a little, and then woke to the sound of someone saying her name quietly and tiptoeing into the room. Carrie was so sick her mind didn't even register the fear and panic she should have had at the thought that someone had come into her house without her knowing about it, but instead simply opened her eyes and tried to focus on who was standing next to her bed.

"Neil?" she finally managed to croak out. "What are you doing here? I'm sick. You shouldn't be here. I don't want you to get sick too."

She saw his large hand reach down and rest lightly on her forehead. His hand felt so cold—so much cooler than she felt. His touch was heavenly.

"Carrie, you're burning up! I'm taking you to the walk-in clinic. No argument."

Trying to shake her head without making herself sick, she turned away. "Leave me alone, Neil. I'm so sick; I just want to sleep."

But Neil wouldn't give up and didn't go away. She watched him rummage around in her closet long enough to find her some sweat pants and a tee shirt to put on, dug under the bed for her flip-flops, and then told her to get dressed and he would be right back. Carrie didn't want to get out of her bed, but knew as sick as she felt, Neil was right; she needed to get checked out by a doctor, so she finally got out of bed and struggled to get dressed. She was trying to run a brush through her tangled locks of hair with her shaking hand when he came back in the room. She finally gave up and pulled the snarled mess into a pony tail. Groaning at how bad she felt and how awful she must look, she trailed after him out of the room. She couldn't believe how weak she was.

If he never wanted to talk to her again after this, she wouldn't blame him. He had definitely seen her at her worst.

She dozed a little in his car on the way to town and was thankful when the doctor in the walk-in clinic was able to see her right away. It didn't take him long to check her over after she was called back to the examining room. He diagnosed a bad case of strep throat, and told her she was very dehydrated and needed to eat and drink or she was going to end up in the hospital. As she struggled to hold her head up, Carrie thought having to be in the hospital didn't sound all bad. The way she felt, dying didn't sound all that bad either.

The doctor gave her a couple of prescriptions to get filled and sent her on her way. By that time she was so exhausted and sick, she didn't care what they did with her. Neil, bless his heart, got her back into the car and drove quickly to the pharmacy where he filled the prescriptions for her. Carrie saw him glance over at her several times on the trip back to the cabin and was touched by the concern on his face. When they got back to her cabin, he saw to it she ate a little something, and made her take her medicine. Then and only then did he allow her to sink back into the comfort of her bed where she immediately fell into an exhausted sleep.

∧∧∧∧∧∧

Neil quietly crept out of Carrie's bedroom, pulled the door shut to where it was only open a crack, and went back to the kitchen to clean up the remains of Carrie's dinner. He hadn't been able to get her to eat more than just a bite or two of toast, but she had finally taken several swallows of orange juice. He wiped everything down quickly with a couple of disinfectant sheets he found in a canister on the kitchen counter, then washed his hands thoroughly with soap and hot water.

Standing in the middle of the living room, he took a deep breath and exhaled while he tried to decide what to do next. It had terrified him to find her so ill. And as sick as she was, he didn't feel he could leave her alone right now. And because of Myrtle's age, there was no way Carrie could go stay with her and bring the germs into her house.

He finally came to a decision, pulled his cell phone out of his pocket, and stepped out on the cabin's front porch to make his call.

"Myrtle, it's Neil. Just wanted you to know I took her to the doctor and got her some meds. She ate and drank a little bit when we got back to the cabin so I could give her the meds the doctor prescribed. She's sleeping now."

"No, I don't think that would be a good idea." He shook his head from side to side as Carrie's aunt tried to convince him to bring Carrie down to her house. "I know you want to take care of her, Miss Myrtle, but you've got yourself and the business to think about. The doctor says strep throat is very contagious, and I sure don't want to you to get it."

He sighed at the worry in Carrie's aunt's voice. "I'm fine. I just wanted you to know that I'm going to spend the night here on the couch so she won't be by herself. That way if she gets worse during the night, I can take her right to the hospital."

"Prayers are appreciated. I'm sure she'll be better in the morning though. Yeah, I'm glad you called me to let me know about her; she was pretty sick when I got here."

Neil finally finished his phone call with Myrtle and stepped back into the cabin, closing the door quietly so he wouldn't disturb Carrie.

As he glanced around the cabin, he felt a restlessness sweep over him. Now he wished he'd brought a book or something with him, but when he'd gotten the frantic phone call from Myrtle that Carrie had called and sounded very sick, he hadn't bothered to grab anything before he left his house.

He'd only taken the time to make one phone call to Patty Jackson, the young woman who worked for him part-time, and asked her to run the store for him today. He hadn't had any idea at the time if he would be able to get there at all today or not, so he was doubly glad now he'd called her.

When he'd arrived at the cabin and let himself in with Myrtle's spare key, he had been dismayed to find Carrie so sick. At first, he wasn't even sure if she recognized him, and when he'd touched her forehead and discovered how high her fever was, he had almost panicked. Thank goodness there was a walk-in clinic in town where he could take her and get her some medicine. The clinic doctor had been right; by tomorrow, she would have probably been so sick she would have ended up in the hospital.

Thank you, Lord, for having Myrtle call me. Please touch Carrie and heal her quickly. She looks so sick, Lord.

He frowned at the thought of how ill she had been. His emotions at the sight of her pale face and fevered eyes had terrified him.

When had she come to mean so much to him?

After standing in the middle of the living room for a moment, Neil finally plopped down on the couch and slipped off his shoes, then leaned back into the cushions and pillows. It was too early for him to go to sleep, but he wanted to be quiet so he didn't disturb Carrie's slumber. Sleep would be good for her right now as her body tried to fight off the infection.

He sat back up and glanced down at the stacks of papers sitting on the table in front of the couch. It looked like Carrie had printed something off her computer. He picked up the stack of papers and started shuffling through the pages.

Mountain Roots, the title sheet said, *by Carolyn E. Montgomery*

Hmmm. Maybe this was the family history she'd told him about.

After skimming through the first few pages, Neil settled himself more comfortably on the couch and put his stocking feet up on the low table in front of him. It didn't take long before he was totally engrossed in the story of two families who lived in Cades Cove, surrounded by the beauty of the Smoky Mountains, and working hard to provide for their families. There were photos—old black and white ones—interspersed throughout the writing; obvious photos of her family members, neighbors, and there were some of scenes long vanished from the Cove. Cabins and farm buildings that had been torn down to make the park what it was today were suddenly brought back to life in the pages before him. The book moved from distant past days to a time in the 1930's when the people of the Cove had been forced to leave because the land had been bought up to become a part of the Great Smoky Mountain National Park.

Then the stories and photos she shared moved to her direct family, this farm, and the cabin he was sitting in, and Neil found himself chuckling as she recounted Myrtle's memories of when she and Jasper Meyers had first settled here. Carrie had even added a few of her own memories—more current—of the farm and her many childhood summers spent here. There were photos of a young Carrie, her beautiful long blond hair hanging in braids over her shoulders as she helped her Uncle Jasper paint fence and do various other chores around the farm. He grinned at the pictures. She had been a cutie even back then. He felt a tug at his heart as he wished he'd been able to know her when she'd been a youngster.

By the time Neil came to the end of the book, which was not yet finished, it was late and he was having a difficult time keeping his eyes open. He tiptoed over to Carrie's bedroom door to check on her one more time, and when he found she was still sleeping soundly, he yawned. Time for him to get some shut-eye too.

Locking both outside doors and turning off all the lights, he said another quick prayer for Carrie's health and spread his long and weary body out on the couch and closed his eyes.

∧∧∧∧∧

Carrie slowly opened her eyes and groaned, feeling like she'd been run over by a truck. Every bone in her body hurt and her throat was still sore, but at least it didn't feel as if it was on fire anymore. Yesterday she'd felt so terrible she had been sure she was going to die right there in her bed. If it hadn't been for Neil Johnston coming and forcing her to go to the doctor, she might have. She smiled a little as she remembered him scolding her for not eating more of her toast yesterday after they returned from the doctor's office. Something told her he would make a wonderful father and it had made her heart feel good to know he cared enough about her to fuss over her health. It had been a long time since anyone had cared about her that much.

She stretched, walked on wobbly legs to the bathroom, and had just made it back to her bed, when she heard the front door lock click and a deep voice call out quietly.

"Carrie, are you awake?"

Neil was back. He must have borrowed the key from Aunt Myrtle—that was how he'd been able to get in the door yesterday. She hadn't even thought about it until now; that's how ill she'd been.

"Yes," she finally squeaked out, and quickly pulled the covers back up around her—although why she was worried about him seeing her in her current state, she didn't know.

He'd already seen her yesterday when she was the sickest, so what did it matter now?

She glanced toward the door and saw him standing there, a large and healthy looking male, with a grin on his face and a couple of paper sacks in his hand.

"Aunt Myrtle sent you some food. Do you want to start with the chicken soup, or the lemon sherbet?"

Carrie laughed, then grimaced at the shooting pain through her throat and neck. "Lemon sherbet sounds heavenly."

Giving her a nod, he turned away. "I'll be right back."

A few moments later he was back with a glass filled with water in one hand and a huge bowl of icy cold sherbet in the other. He handed her the glass first, put the bowl on the bedside table, and pulled a couple of medicine bottles out of the pocket of his jeans.

"First you have to take your medicine though. Then you get your sherbet."

She stuck her tongue out at him playfully and smiled. "You are so bossy!" she croaked.

Carrie dutifully took the meds he gave her, drank the water, and then pulled herself up to sit propped up against the headboard and waited patiently until he handed her the bowl of sherbet. She moaned in appreciation as the first spoonful slid down and soothed her fiery throat.

"Oh, this is so good, Neil. Thank you."

"You're welcome," Neil stated. "I'll be back."

He left the room and Carrie concentrated on enjoying each spoonful of the lemon tastiness as it comforted her throat. Her Aunt Myrtie was an angel to send this to her, and Neil Johnston was her hero for bringing it.

All too soon Carrie was scraping the last of her icy treat from the bottom of her bowl, the spoon making a squeaky sound as she tried to get every morsel of it. She reached over to place the empty bowl on the bedside stand and curled back up under the covers. Neil hadn't returned yet, but she could hear him banging around in the kitchen. Maybe she'd just close her eyes for a time while she waited.

She was sure she hadn't been sleeping long at all when Neil came back into the room, waking her up when he cleared his throat. Carrie opened her eyes and saw him standing at the edge of the bed with a tray covered with a dishtowel. She pulled herself back up against the headboard and struggled to open her eyes.

"I was snoozing," she mumbled.

He gave a little chuckle. "I noticed." He placed the laden tray on her lap. "You eat some of this and then I promise I'll leave you alone and let you sleep. Deal?"

Carrie looked at the tray. There was a bowl of her Aunt Myrtle's chicken noodle soup, the aroma of it tantalizing her taste buds. Neil had also placed a napkin and spoon on the tray. But what shocked her most was the white vase with a single red rose in it. She looked up at him in surprise.

"Thank you, Neil. This is so nice of you."

He smiled at her gently. "You're a friend. Friends take care of each other."

Carrie tried to swallow back her emotion, then nodded, and picked up the spoon to tentatively take a sip of the hot soup. It was so good.

"Mmm. Aunt Myrtle makes the best chicken soup."

She heard another low chuckle from him and wondered what she had said that was so funny.

"Your Aunt Myrtle makes the best everything, Carrie. Haven't you figured that out yet?"

She grinned up at him and nodded. He was right, of course.

He stood there at the side of her bed and looked down at her for a moment. Carrie couldn't help but notice how weary he looked. Had he slept at all the night before? Then a thought hit her.

"Did you stay here all last night?" She didn't know why the thought of a strange man being here in the cabin with her didn't send her into a panic like it would have once upon a time, but instead of fear, she felt nothing but safety and comfort when Neil was nearby.

"I stayed most of the night—I slept a little—on the couch." He frowned. "I was really worried about you and didn't want to leave you alone in case you got worse."

She saw him take a deep breath and reach up with his right hand to push his hair off his forehead. "But, seeing as how you're doing much better this morning, and now that I've delivered the food from your Aunt Myrtle as ordered by her...if you think you'll be okay...."

"Oh," she nodded her head, suddenly understanding. "Of course, I'll be fine. You have a business to run. But thank you so much for all you did for me."

"No problem." He turned toward the door. "I'll see myself out then." He stopped with his right hand on the door jamb. "But if you get worse or need anything at all, please call me, Carrie." His brown eyes were serious as they locked with hers from across the room. "I mean it, okay?"

She nodded, feeling unnerved by the intense look in his eyes and the huskiness in his voice. "I will, I promise. And thank you again, Neil."

He nodded, looked at her for a moment more, and then turned to leave, his voice called out as he left. "Rest and get better, Carrie Montgomery. I still have a lot of Tennessee to show you!"

As Carrie heard the front door close, she grinned and turned her attention back to her bowl of soup, the sight of the red rose on her tray cheering her.

Being sick wasn't fun, but Neil made it almost a pleasure. And the thought of spending more time with the handsome man who had just left the cabin, filled her with expectation. Maybe he was starting to feel more than just friendship toward her after all.

She couldn't get well fast enough.

∧∧∧∧∧∧

Carrie spent the next few days recuperating at the cabin. She ate, she drank plenty of fluids, and took the rest of the antibiotic the doctor had prescribed her. She also spent hours reading her great-grandpa's old Bible. He had underlined hundreds of passages that had evidently meant something to him, and Carrie scoured through the pages of the old book, searching for answers to her many questions. Ever since the Passion Play she had felt the need to go back to reading the Bible, searching for the faith of her childhood. So many of the verses underlined in the Bible spoke to her, as if they were just for her:

...But this one thing I do, forgetting those things which are behind, and reaching forth unto those things which are before. (Philippians 3:13b)

Peace I leave with you, my peace I give unto you: not as the world giveth, give I unto you. Let not your heart be troubled, neither let it be afraid. (John 14:27)

And the peace of God, which passeth all understanding, shall keep your hearts and minds through Christ Jesus. (Philippians 4:7)

For ye shall go out with joy, and be led forth with peace: the mountains and the hills shall break forth before you into singing, and all the trees of the field shall clap their hands. (Isaiah 55:12)

Peace and joy were things Lloyd Taylor had taken from her, but with God's help, Carrie intended to get them back.

While she'd been sick, she'd received a packet of forwarded mail from her roommate in Lexington. She had almost cried when she'd found a large manila envelope in the packet from her school, filled with hand-made cards from her former second grade students. With her being ill, the timing for receiving them had been perfect. Carrie had laughed and cried as she read the cards they'd each created with love. Oh, how she missed her children. They weren't always easy to deal with, but they had been her responsibility for almost an entire school year. It made her sad to realize that when she returned to the classroom in the fall, she wouldn't be teaching these same children. They would have moved on to third grade; and she'd be starting all over again with a fresh batch. But she loved it.

Carrie was also surprised to find another large envelope from the District Attorney. Then she remembered the phone call from the DA, telling her she would be sending her the letter from Lloyd Taylor. She held the envelope in her hands for a while and just stared at it before finally taking a deep breath and tearing it open.

If she were going to leave everything in God's hands, this was an opportunity for her to step out in faith. She had to start somewhere.

The DA had written a letter to her explaining that the smaller envelope in the packet held a letter from Lloyd Taylor, the man who had attacked her. At first Carrie had stuffed it back into the larger envelope without reading it. But curiosity finally won out and she pulled it back out and carefully slit it open with her letter opener.

It was a hand-written letter on simple lined white notebook paper, the handwriting more printing than cursive, and it definitely looked like a man had written it. Carrie tried to approach reading it as if she didn't know who it was from, hoping that would help her deal with the myriad of emotions that swept through her as she held it in her hands.

Miss Montgomery,

I don't even know how to write this letter. When I think of what I did to you—what I could have done to you if your roommate hadn't come home when she did—I am horrified. Now that I am on meds here in prison, I realize I don't even remember who I was when I stalked and attacked you.

But that doesn't make me any less responsible for what I did. Because of this, I contacted the parole board and told them I don't want to be considered for early parole—even if I was eligible for it. I'm going to serve my whole sentence. Even that doesn't seem like enough for what I did to you. There is no way to make it up to you.

I want you to know I'm a changed man. During my time here in prison I have become friends with the prison chaplain, and he led me to know Christ as my personal savior several months ago. Knowing God loved someone as bad as me enough to send His son to die on the cross for MY sins, is almost more than I can wrap my head around. I won't ever feel like I deserve that forgiveness.

Which brings me to the reason for this letter. I talked to our attorneys and told them I wanted to send you this letter. At first, they didn't want to allow it and I guess I don't blame them. They didn't want to put you through any more pain than you've already been through. So, for a while I forgot about it.

> *But I've been praying about it more and more, and God convicted me that this is something I have to do, so with our attorneys' approval, I'm writing you this letter. I want you to know I'm not sending it for me. I'm sending it for you.*
>
> *The Lord has put on my heart that I am supposed to tell you how sorry I am for what I did to you. I don't really feel you should ever forgive me. But then, I'm not worthy of forgiveness from God either, and yet He did forgive me.*
>
> *I also wanted to promise you something: I promise you, Miss Montgomery, you don't ever have to be afraid of me again. Even when I am released – 20 years or so from now – I will NEVER make any attempt to contact you. I will never do anything to hurt you again—I promise you that.*
>
> *I don't want you to live in fear for the rest of your life because of what I did to you. Please, allow yourself to have a good life—the life God wants you to live.*
>
> *"And ye shall know the truth, and the truth shall make you free." – John 8:32*
>
> *Sincerely,*
> *Lloyd Taylor*

Carrie sobbed while she read the letter. She didn't know why, but she really felt the man was being sincere. She hoped for his sake he had really made the decision to turn his life over to God and start over. The fact that he was refusing any possibility for early parole made a bigger impact on her than any other part of the letter. And his promise to her that she need never fear him again released some of the old terrors from her mind.

She prayed he was telling her the truth in the letter. It would be so wonderful to be free of the fear she'd been living with for the past year.

Maybe she wasn't ready to forgive him today, but someday, somewhere down the road, she hoped she would be. A part of her understood that until she totally forgave him for what he had done to her, she would be as much imprisoned as he was.

CHAPTER 12

It was Wednesday the following week before Carrie physically began to feel like herself again. She still didn't have as much energy as she'd had before she'd fallen ill, but was sleeping well and feeling a little bit stronger every morning. Even though Aunt Myrtie protested, Carrie finally went back to work at the restaurant on Thursday morning, one week from the day Neil had found her in the cabin, burning up with a fever. She hadn't seen him since he'd left the cabin that next day, but he'd called her every evening to check up on her, and they usually spent at least half an hour on the phone, chatting about how their day had gone.

Carrie had told Dr. Susan Martin about her attraction to Neil during one of their weekly sessions. Susan had cautioned her about getting too attached to him if he was still in the process of getting over his wife's death. She also reminded Carrie she was leaving Tennessee in a few months. Carrie didn't need to have a therapist tell her to be careful, but her heart wanted what it wanted, and she was powerless to control her feelings when Neil Johnston was concerned.

He'd already invited her to go back to the Cove with him the upcoming Saturday. At first she hadn't been sure if she should accept—not because she didn't want to spend the time with him—but because she wasn't sure how strong she would be after working two days at *Meyers Place*. But Saturday morning she'd awakened feeling more like her old self than she had in over a week.

She quickly showered and dressed, this time in a sleeveless light blue cotton shirt and khaki colored shorts, along with heavier cotton socks and her hiking boots. After eating a hearty breakfast, she packed the cooler with a luncheon for the two of them, then grabbed her camera and purse and went out on the front porch of the cabin to wait for his arrival. She was excited—and even a little nervous. Sometime during the last week—ever since she'd been sick—their relationship had changed. There was a different level of friendship between them now, and she was both anxious and curious to see where it would lead. Even though in the back of her mind was the realization that in eight weeks she would be leaving to go back to her job and real life in the city, she couldn't help herself.

And the more she thought about it all, the less Carrie looked forward to going home.

When her boyfriend of two years, Sean McCavit, broke off their relationship after the attack, Carrie had been heartbroken and had felt his rejection was like an additional stab in the heart. She had thought their two-year relationship was starting to get serious, and was sure he was going to pop 'the question'—soon. Then he'd told her he thought it was best if they didn't see each other anymore. She knew he'd been hurt when she'd pulled away—both emotionally and physically—from him after she was attacked. She couldn't even stand to have him hold her hand anymore—let alone kiss her. Whenever he touched her, all she could think of was what it had felt like when she'd been brutally manhandled and beaten by Lloyd Taylor. The last time she had cowered from Sean's touch, he had thrown his hands up in the air and walked away from her. The next day he had called her and said he thought it was best if they didn't see each other anymore. He hadn't come right out and blamed her for the end of their relationship, but it was obvious to Carrie that he felt she was at fault.

After all she'd suffered after the attack—the need to heal physically, the stress of having to deal with the questions, both personal and professional in the courtroom—almost as if she were on trial instead of the man who had almost killed her—when Sean had told her he was finished with her, it had felt like the final straw.

Looking back on it now, it wasn't surprising she had spent most of her days silently weeping. There had been talk at school between the other teachers and many complaints from the parents, and when the principal and superintendent of schools had called her into the administrative office to discuss the situation with her, she had almost been relieved to not have to face her fellow-employees and acquaintances anymore. It had been more than she could mentally handle right then. Her psyche was so brittle, she felt as if it wouldn't take much for her to completely shatter.

But something was happening to her here in the mountains. It was as if she had been re-born as a stronger, more grounded individual. Maybe it was because she had spent so much time reading and writing about the stories of her ancestors. After seeing what they had survived and the struggles they had withstood to settle this country, how could she sit around feeling sorry for herself?

Perhaps it was partially due to her weekly sessions with Sue Martin. The other young woman had been able to reach her in a way that no one else had, and had forced her into coming to grips with the attack and how she had responded to it. Carrie had finally been able to see that she hadn't done anything to lead Lloyd Taylor into what he'd done to her. She had just been a victim. Susan had prayed with her at the end of each session, and Carrie was thankful for having had her to talk with through the summer.

However, Carrie believed the majority of her strength came from her renewed relationship with God. During her convalescence she'd read portions of the Bible she hadn't taken the time to read since her childhood. The verses she read reminded her of the truth she had learned so many years ago during a vacation bible school; God loved her enough He'd sent his only Son to die on the cross for her sins. She'd made a decision that summer to accept Christ as her own personal savior, and had even been baptized.

Then her Aunt Myrtle reminded her one night after a dinner, that it wasn't about having religion. It was about having a personal relationship with Christ. Somewhere along the line, Carrie had forgotten that basic truth—that simple knowledge. Once upon a time, Jesus had been her best friend in the whole world and she had trusted in His will completely. When she'd become so wrapped up in college life and having a career and making friends, she'd lost that relationship with her savior.

Coming back to her roots had renewed her faith and she'd found that special relationship again, and she never wanted to lose it.

It was time for her to get on with her life. True, she only had a couple precious months here remaining, but she was going to enjoy each and every day of it, and when the time came to go back home, she would go back with her head held high.

She held tightly to two of the verses she'd found underlined in her great-grandfather's old Bible.

> The first one was from Jeremiah, chapter 29 and verse 11: *For I know the thoughts that I think toward you, saith the Lord, thoughts of peace, and not of evil, to give you hope.*

And from Psalm, chapter 27; *Wait on the Lord: be of good courage, and he shall strengthen thine heart: wait, I say, on the Lord.*

And her favorite from John 14, verse 29: *Peace I leave with you; my peace I give unto you: not as the world giveth, give I unto you. Let not your heart be troubled, neither let it be afraid.*

So she was trying to have hope…and waiting—patiently—to see what the Lord had in store for her next. He'd gotten her through the past year; He could surely be trusted to take care of whatever was ahead of her in life.

Carrie heard the sound of car tires crunching drift up the side of the mountain and knew Neil was on his way up the gravel drive to the cabin. The excitement that coursed through her took her by surprise. Was she crazy? She had to get her emotions under control. The last thing she needed was to fall in love with this man. She took a deep breath and tried to slow her heartbeat. Today needed to be thought of as a day spent with a friend.

That was all.

∧∧∧∧∧∧

Neil knew there was a silly grin on his face as he drove around the last curve of the steep driveway and the cabin came into view. He couldn't believe how much he had looked forward to this day.

Carrie already sat on the top step of the porch waiting for him. It made him feel good to know she was as excited about going with him today as he was to have her go with him. He'd made arrangements to have Patty run the gallery again today so he could spend the whole day with Carrie and not have to worry about business. In the back of his mind was the knowledge that the clock was ticking and Carrie would be leaving before he knew it. But today, he was not going to think about that. Today was all about having a good time with a very good friend.

Before he had even opened his car door, Carrie had bounded off the steps and was standing in front of him.

"I made lunch for us again," she stated almost breathlessly. She was lovely this morning, the light azure of her shirt bringing out the blueness of her eyes even more than usual. Who was he kidding? He thought she was beautiful every day. Even when she'd been ill and he'd seen her with sweaty hair and disheveled clothes, as far as he was concerned, she had been the loveliest woman in the world.

He gulped as his thoughts briefly turned to Lisa. Once upon a time he had thought she was the most beautiful woman in the world. He turned his mind from the past and gave Carrie a smile.

"I look forward to it," he finally said as he grabbed the cooler from her and put it on the floor in the back seat of his vehicle.

He watched her hurry around the vehicle and get in the passenger side, pushing a stray hair or two out of her eyes. Taking a deep breath, he rushed to get back in the car so they could get going. There just weren't enough hours in the day when he was with her.

Neil took his time driving to the Cove while Carrie chatted about her days at the restaurant and he told her about his latest painting. He also shared his excitement about a commission he'd recently received from a well-to-do businessman in Chicago for several framed watercolors of the Smoky Mountain area. The man was a former client of Neil's from when he worked in the law firm. Neil didn't do a great many watercolors, but he could hardly wait to get started on these; but first this trip was necessary for inspiration and ideas. He'd brought along his camera and a sketch pad and hoped to get enough sketches to use for the paintings.

When they reached the Cove, they drove by the buildings they had previously seen until they came to the John P. Cable Mill, a working grist mill. Neil was always fascinated by the flume which took the water to the huge waterwheel which in turn provided the power to turn the huge stones inside the mill that ground the corn into corn meal. While he sat on a rock outside the mill and drew sketches, Carrie wandered into the building to talk to the elderly gentlemen running the mill. Neil wasn't surprised when Carrie didn't come back out for fifteen minutes or more. He had to chuckle a little as he worked on another sketch. It was obvious she'd found someone from which to glean more stories of the Cove.

While he waited outside for Carrie, Neil took the opportunity to do meticulous pencil sketches of both the mill and the nearby Becky Cable House. He remembered from his reading about the area that the house had also been used as a general store for many years. Becky lived in the house until her death in 1940 in her mid-nineties. From the stories he'd heard, Becky Cable had been a single woman who had not only taken care of herself her whole life, but had also taken care of those around her, including many nieces and nephews. Neil found the house particularly pleasing architecturally because of the hand-made wooden shingles and the wide covered porch.

After they left the mill area, Neil and Carrie drove on down the road to the Henry Whitehead place. It broke Neil's heart to see what vandals had done to the lovely cabin over the years. People had carved their names and other not so nice things into the logs and even the mantel of the fireplace inside the house. It was a shame to see how little some people appreciated history.

The cabin itself was a work of art though. Neil had read that Henry had built it for his wife, Matilda, in 1898. It was easily one of the nicest log homes in the Cove with a beautiful brick chimney—a rarity back then. Neil also appreciated the craftsmanship it must have taken Henry to build the cabin as it was made of square-sawed logs that were finished smooth inside the cabin. It was probably much warmer for Henry and his family than the other cabins too as it had walls that looked to be at least four inch thick with practically no spaces between the logs. Neil spent a while sketching the cabin and Carrie gave him plenty of time to do so as she meandered through and around the cabin, taking photos with her camera.

Neil also snapped several photos of some of the wildflowers in the nearby wooded area and fields. He had learned several of their names over the years; the blue of Monk's Hood, the bright yellow coneflowers, red bee-balm, and purple passion flowers. The beauty of the Cove never ceased to amaze him.

After he and Carrie wandered around for about half an hour, they finally made their way down the road to the next stop—the Dan Lawson cabin, and then on to the Tipton place, and from there to the Carter Shields cabin, which was Neil's favorite of all the old homesteads in the Cove. There was just something about the way the cabin sat nestled in the woods with the mountains behind it; it made it feel homier than some of the others. Neil had heard that Carter had been crippled in the Battle of Shiloh during the Civil War, but came to live out his days in this beautiful spot with the dogwood trees blooming in the spring and the tall leafy trees shading the cabin from the summer's hot sun. Neil had probably taken more photos of this cabin than anything else in the Cove, but today he was here to do sketches. As soon as he finished up his sketch of the cabin though, he quickly flipped to the next sheet of paper in his tablet and started sketching again. This time though, he sketched Carrie, standing on the front porch with her hand on the post, looking out toward the surrounding forests and hills as if daydreaming. Today, with her blond hair pulled back with a clip at her neck, and a few wisps blowing around her face, he thought she looked like an angel.

He quickly finished the sketch, lifted his camera from around his neck and also took a few shots of her standing on the cabin porch, then the yard and woods around the cabin. For some reason, it was important to him to be able to recall this particular spot, this moment, and this day. He wanted to remember how it felt to have someone to spend a day with, somebody who didn't ask anything from him other than to just be there. It had been way too many years since he'd had a special someone to share a day with like this.

Someone like Carrie.

∧∧∧∧∧

After they ate their lunch at a camping spot in the Park, Neil drove his vehicle out of the Cove and headed toward the Foothills Parkway. He saw Carrie turn to look at him from the passenger side of the car, a questioning look on her face.

"There's one more place I want to show you," he told her with a small smile on his face.

She gave him a nod and he turned his attention back to the curves in the road. As he drove, he thought about how much it meant to him that she trusted him enough that she hadn't even asked where they were going. He was sure that wouldn't have been the case when she had first arrived in Tennessee.

Because she'd spent so many of her summers here, he knew she had probably been to his favorite spot sometime in the past, but today he wanted to share it with her. He wanted to see her eyes as she looked out on the view he had come to love.

They drove about fifteen minutes and then arrived at the lookout spot he was searching for and pulled the car over and parked. He watched as Carrie slowly opened her car door and got out of the car, then walked over to the edge of the parking area. Neil smiled as he recognized the look of awe that swept over her face.

He knew the feeling.

∧∧∧∧∧

Carrie gazed out over the scene before her, feeling a slight moment of vertigo when she realized how far the valley was below them. Then she raised her eyes again to the mountains in the distance—mountain range after range after range spread out before them. There was the ever-present misty blue haze and there were a few clouds, but the fog of the morning had cleared enough that the view was unending. In the valley below her, she could just make out a small house and what looked like the steeple on a white framed church near it.

She felt Neil's presence beside her and turned to give him a grin.

"This is...awesome!" she finally spit out, at a loss for a better word to describe how she felt.

Neil gave a little chuckle and grinned back at her. "I'm so glad you like it. This is one of my most favorite spots in this area. I've probably taken hundreds of photos at this very location—maybe thousands. I could stand right here for the rest of my life and be perfectly happy."

Carrie caught her breath as Neil suddenly moved close to her and put his right arm across her shoulders and pulled her up against his side. She could smell his spicy aftershave and felt his warm breath on her face when she turned her face to the left enough to look at him. What surprised her most though was the realization that she wasn't afraid of him and didn't feel like automatically pulling away from his touch the way she had flinched whenever Sean had tried to touch her.

He lifted his left arm and pointed.

"That mountain range right there…" her eyes followed his pointing fingers. "That is Mount Le Conte. It's about twenty four miles from here."

His arm and hand moved to the next mountain range as he continued. "Then comes Clingman's Dome, which is about twenty three miles away. It's the highest of these mountain ranges in front of us." He turned his face a little and grinned at her. He was so close she could see the little flecks of gold in his dark brown eyes. For a moment she was mesmerized and almost forgot to breathe.

"If you've never been to the top of Clingman's Dome and looked out on the mountain ranges all around you, it's something you should do sometime. Just dress warm. Even in the summer, it's cold up there."

Carrie automatically nodded, not really sure what he had just told her. She was too busy concentrating on the fact that he still had his arm around her and she was enjoying it.

A lot.

Neil turned his head to look back at the vista in front of them and Carrie turned her eyes back to the mountains too, trying to catch her breath. With his face so close to hers, she almost forgot about the view.

"Then we have Thunderhead Mountain which rests about thirteen miles from here, then Rich Mountain which is the closest to us at about six and a half miles away."

Her eyes followed his arm and pointing hand. "Behind those ridges right there sits Cades Cove—about eight miles away; then Gregory Bald which is about thirteen miles from here."

She felt him take a deep breath. "And there, Miss Montgomery, is the best view of the mountains you'll find around here; at least, that's my opinion."

Neil moved his arm from her shoulders and took a step away and Carrie felt for a moment like she might fall without his support, then caught herself. She concentrated on the mountains and the view in front of her and attempted to settle her heartbeat. The vertigo she was feeling now didn't have anything to do with heights; it had everything to do with the man beside her.

She was afraid—not of him—but of what she was starting to feel toward him. It was a different type of fear, for certain; but scary nonetheless.

But as the feelings raced through her, she finally knew she had to accept the truth; what she felt for Neil Johnston was much more than a simple friendship.

So much more.

CHAPTER 13

Neil stepped back from Carrie after moving his arm from her shoulders, feeling something that surprised him. After losing his wife, Lisa, he had been positive he would never feel a strong attraction for another woman. He had dated several women over the years since his wife's death and had never felt the same attraction he had felt for his wife. Then Carrie Montgomery had appeared in his gallery and his world had shifted, and now he was having feelings for this woman that confused him. There was a connection between the two of them, but a part of him realized he wasn't ready for what was happening in his heart.

He'd tried to convince himself they were just friends, but he was beginning to wonder about that. They talked on the phone almost every night and he looked forward more than he wanted to admit to excursions like today. When he had his arm around her shoulders moments before, he had been drawn to pull her into his arms like he had the day at the waterfall. Sure, that day he had just wanted to comfort her. But today—today, he wanted to hold her because he enjoyed having her in his arms. And he couldn't help but wonder what it would be like to kiss her.

And it terrified him. Was he ready for another relationship?

Carrie turned her face back to him and there was almost an expectant look on her face as his gaze locked on her sparkling blue eyes. She looked at him with such...he wasn't sure what the look was; but before he realized what he was planning to do, he took a step closer to her and saw her tip up her face a little further. He slowly reached out and cupped her face with his hands to pull her toward him, then leaned down to place his lips on hers for a kiss. Her lips were so soft and sweet; for a few seconds he was lost in the moment, enjoying the taste of her as the rest of the world melted away around them. Then reality came crashing down and he pulled away from her.

What was he thinking?

He gulped, glanced down at her flushed face, and watched her eyes fly open. He quickly looked away and took a couple of deeps breaths to slow down his racing emotions. He couldn't believe he'd done that.

On the other hand, he shouldn't have been surprised. Ever since he'd first seen her, he'd been drawn to her in an unexplained way.

Fortunately, Carrie didn't seem to notice his awkwardness after the kiss, or if she did, she was graceful enough to ignore it as she continued to comment on the beautiful views. Meanwhile Neil's mind felt like scrambled eggs as he tried to catch his breath and deal with his roller coaster emotions.

It was ridiculous for him to think they were ever going to be more than just friends. After all, she was leaving in a couple of months—headed back to her life in the city. He never should have crossed over that invisible line and kissed her. He had nothing to offer her. After all, his heart still belonged to Lisa.

Hopefully he hadn't permanently damaged their friendship by his impulsive move.

All he knew was, he needed to back away from her for a while. To anyone looking on their relationship from the outside it probably appeared he was pursuing her. After all, he sat next to her every Sunday in church, they talked on the phone almost every evening, and now he'd kissed her. What kind of message was he sending to Carrie by his actions?

He had never meant to do anything to cause her more pain. She'd already been through more than any woman should have to go through.

Lord, I didn't mean to do anything to hurt her. Should I apologize to her? I'm not really sorry I kissed her—yet I don't want her to get the wrong idea....

The two of them got back in the vehicle with Carrie continuing to gush about how beautiful the mountains were and thanking him again for bringing her here. Neil only listened with one ear while his mind struggled with his conflicting emotions.

He liked being around Carrie—really liked spending time with her and talking with her. But he didn't think he was ready for anything beyond friendship, and until he was, he needed to put some space between the two of them before one of them—if not both—ended up getting hurt.

Unless it was already too late.

∧∧∧∧∧∧

The closer they got to Carrie's cabin, the quieter it became in the vehicle. As far as Carrie was concerned, things had changed between them since Neil had kissed her. She had been totally taken by surprise when he had pulled her into that passionate kiss. She had been shocked by his actions, but had found herself greatly enjoying the moment— a lot. She hadn't been repulsed like she had been with Sean after the attack and that had surprised Carrie even more than the kiss itself.

It had caused her a great deal of joy to know she could still respond to a man with something other than fear, as there had been a point in her life not that long ago when she hadn't been sure she ever would. But she wasn't sure what to make of Neil's actions. Did the kiss mean Neil was starting to have romantic feelings toward her? She had thought they were just friends. Before today, he'd never given her the impression that he thought of her as anything more than a pal—someone to hang around with. And to further complicate matters, it wasn't going to be long and she would be going back to her real life. She certainly didn't want to leave someone behind that she'd hurt because she wasn't ready for a more serious relationship.

So what did it all mean?

She chewed on her lower lip as she gazed out the window at the passing scenery. For weeks she'd told herself to be careful of her heart. The more time she'd spent with Neil, the more they talked on the phone, the more she knew the truth. It was too late. She'd already fallen in love with this wonderful man beside her.

However, in only a few weeks, she'd be leaving to return to her job and life in the city. It would be foolish for her to get any more involved with him than she already had. Maybe the best thing for both of them would be for her to back away now before one or both of them got hurt.

If she didn't, she was going to lose her heart to him forever.

∧∧∧∧∧

The next day being a Sunday, Carrie expected Neil to come and sit in the pew next to her like he had all the previous Sundays. When the service started and he didn't appear, she let out a sigh of resignation. He wasn't coming. She didn't know whether to be relieved or disappointed. At least she wouldn't have to feel embarrassed and uncomfortable about yesterday's kiss.

Aunt Myrtle was quiet on the trip home and Carrie was appreciative of the silence in the car. With Carrie's emotions on a roller-coaster ride, she didn't know what her reaction would have been if her aunt had brought up the subject of Neil's absence.

Carrie had replayed the moment Neil had kissed her in the mountains dozens of times in the past twenty four hours. The kiss had left her breathless and flustered, but not because she was afraid of him or repulsed by him. Quite the contrary. As a matter of fact, she hadn't been sure if the feeling of dizziness after he kissed her had been caused by their standing at the edge of the steep mountainside, or if it had been caused by her reaction to his kiss. She was thinking it was more the latter. Neil Johnston made her feel things she had never felt with another man—even Sean. He made her feel cherished and special; he made her believe she was beautiful and worthwhile and desirable.

He made her feel loved.

∧∧∧∧∧∧

The next week flew by as Carrie worked every morning at the restaurant with her aunt. She had become good friends with the other employees—Charlie, Kathy, and Sadie—and found herself actually enjoying the teasing and easy banter between the three of them. Carrie had never had any siblings, and it seemed nice to be a part of a group that clearly enjoyed each other's company as much as those three did. Even though they all worked hard at making the restaurant a great place for people to enjoy a meal, they had a good time together doing it. She didn't know if the rest of them felt that way, but to Carrie, it almost didn't feel like a job.

Charlie had proudly shown her a photo he carried in his wallet of his girlfriend, who worked in Maryville as a secretary for an attorney. They had plans to get married in the spring, and it was obvious by the look of adoration on Charlie's face whenever he talked about his fiancée, Grace, he was truly in love with her. Even though she knew it was wrong, Carrie couldn't help but feel a little jealous. She had thought at one time she had that type of relationship with Sean. But seeing Charlie and Grace together, it was obvious what Sean and she had once had wasn't even close.

Day after day as Carrie drove home after a long day at the restaurant, she would watch the sun-driven heat shimmer across the road and wonder if she would ever have a man to spend the rest of her life with—if she would ever have children to pass the stories of her family along to. It had been days since she'd heard anything from Neil. Once he had kissed her, it was as if he had decided to pull away from her. Obviously, he hadn't been as affected by the kiss as she had been. At first, she had felt hurt; then had straightened her shoulders, lifted her head, and decided it was his loss. She had a great deal of love to give a man. If it wasn't to be Neil, she would just have to trust God would bring the right man to her when it was time. Or if she was supposed to be alone the rest of her life, she'd be okay with that too. She still had her family.

One day Carrie watched a family of parents and three children leave the restaurant and was hit with a realization; she no longer felt as if she had to look on everyone around her as a possible stalker. She wasn't sure when it had happened—maybe after she'd received the letter from Lloyd Taylor—but somewhere along the way, she had lost some of her fear. As the feeling of peace swept over her, she almost yelled in response, but instead just gave a grin to the women at the booth where she was re-filling their coffee cups.

It had been a long wait, but she was healing.

The Healing Hills

∧∧∧∧∧

Several more weeks passed and Carrie felt her life falling into a routine of sorts. As much as she had been unsure about coming here, her remaining time in Tennessee was passing too quickly for Carrie's liking. Before she knew it, it would be the end of summer and time to go home.

Then early one Monday morning Carrie got a phone call from her aunt. Aunt Myrtle hadn't felt well the day before and had even stayed home from church, which was unusual for her. She explained on the phone that she didn't feel well and asked if Carrie would be able to open the restaurant for her that morning.

"Of course I will, Aunt Myrtie. But if you're feeling that bad, maybe you should go to the doctor."

She heard her aunt cough on the other end of the phone. It sounded like Aunt Myrtie was really struggling to get her breath and Carrie felt instant concern for her aunt's health.

"I'll be okay, dearie. I just need some rest. I'll take some aspirin and cough medicine and I'm sure I'll be right as rain in the morning."

But she wasn't. When Carrie stopped by that evening after working all day at *Meyers Place*, her aunt was staggering around the kitchen trying to fix herself a cup of tea. She looked awful, and Carrie felt the cold tendrils of fear as she realized just how sick her dear aunt really was.

"I'm calling your doctor," Carrie stated even while the older woman was shaking her head.

"Their office is already closed, Carrie. I'll call them tomorrow." She coughed and wheezed, and Carrie watched as she slowly sat down in a kitchen chair, her hand shaking as she sat her tea cup on the table.

"Well, as sick as you are, Aunt Myrtle, you can't wait until tomorrow. You need to go to the hospital."

Her aunt waved one hand through the air as she covered her mouth with her other hand and wheezed.

Carrie felt helpless. She knew how stubborn her aunt was. How was she ever going to get her to go to the hospital to get checked out? If she called an ambulance, her aunt could refuse to go with them—besides, Aunt Myrtie would never forgive her. But she had to do something. She finally pulled her phone out of her pocket and dialed the only person she knew she could call for help.

"Neil? I'm sorry to bother you, but Aunt Myrtie is really sick and I need your help."

∧∧∧∧∧

He couldn't deny how relieved he was to finally hear from Carrie—even though the reason she had called him hadn't been good news. He knew when the phone rang this early in the morning, it wasn't a good thing, but he hadn't had any notion it would be about Myrtle. Myrtle Meyers was one of the most stubborn women he had ever met, but if Carrie felt she was sick enough she needed to go to the hospital, then he was going see to it that the precious woman went.

When he arrived at Myrtle's house, Carrie met him at the door. There was no bright smile on her face—only worry and stress.

"She's so sick, Neil," Carrie whispered to him as she let him in through the kitchen door. He followed her to the living room and watched while Carrie kneeled down to finish tying Myrtle's shoes. Myrtle sat, almost reclined, on the couch, her face pale and her eyes glazed over behind her glasses.

"Aunt Myrtie, Neil is here. He's going to help me get you to the car and then we're going to take you to the hospital so they can check you out. Okay?"

Neil saw Myrtle look up at him as if she couldn't quite focus on him. As sick as Carrie had been several weeks earlier, Myrtle was much sicker.

"Do you think she's sick with the same thing you had, Carrie?"

As Carrie turned her blue eyes on him with concern on her face, Neil felt like a fool. Why had he said something like that? Carrie had to be worried to death about her aunt, and then he had to add to it by compounding her worry with guilt?

Myrtle coughed and shook her head. "I don't have strep throat. I just have this cough and my chest feels like there's an elephant sitting on it."

Carrie and Neil helped the weak and ill woman up from the couch and slowly walked out to the car with her between them, both holding onto her arms to hold her up. The drive into town seemed to Neil to take forever, but fortunately when they got to the emergency room at the hospital, they were the only people waiting. While a nurse took Myrtle into an examining room, and Carrie helped fill out paperwork for the billing, Neil sat in the waiting room and prayed for Myrtle's health. He was more concerned than he had let on to Carrie. At Myrtle's age, even a simple case of the flu could end badly.

After completing the billing process, Carrie stepped into the waiting room long enough to let him know she was going back to the examining room to be with her aunt, and he nodded.

"I'll be praying for her, Carrie." He grabbed her hand quickly before she turned to leave. "And I'll be right here waiting if you need me."

She gazed at him with tears in her eyes. "Thanks, Neil. I don't know what I'd do if anything happens to her...."

He quickly shook his head. "She's a strong woman, Carrie. She will be just fine now that she's here where they can treat her."

Carrie slowly nodded, sniffed, and left the room. Neil plopped back down in one of the uncomfortable waiting room chairs and bowed his head. He hated hospitals—hated the smell of them, the sounds of them—the very atmosphere. He'd spent hours in one, waiting while life left his baby girl's body. He didn't blame the doctors or nurses though. He knew there were some things they couldn't do anything about.

The truth was, sometimes all you could do was pray.

CHAPTER 14

Carrie nodded her understanding as the doctor explained to Aunt Myrtle one more time why he was admitting her into the hospital. She totally agreed with his decision to keep her aunt here—at least for a day or two. As sick as Aunt Myrtle had been when she found her at the house, Carrie was terrified of something happening to her.

"I don't want to stay here, Carolyn Elizabeth."

She smiled a little at her aunt's use of her real name. Aunt Myrtie only did that when she was either very happy or very upset. Carrie was perfectly aware that her aunt was not pleased with her right now since she'd been the one who had made the decision to bring her to the hospital. But the doctor needed to do more tests, and that meant Aunt Myrtle was staying put. The doctor told Carrie he was pretty sure her aunt had pneumonia, but because of her age, wanted to run some tests on her heart.

"Aunt Myrtie, you are very sick. Please understand Doctor Belson needs to run some tests and get you on some medication so you'll feel better. Please don't fight us on this. Please."

The elderly woman coughed, then slowly nodded her head in defeat, although she stuck her lower lip out a little bit. Her aunt could be so childish when she didn't get her way.

"Okay, Carrie. Just promise me you'll water my plants and take care of feeding Buster. Oh, and Charlie and you will have to run the restaurant." She sighed. "I don't know how things will get done without me there to see to 'em."

She patted Aunt Myrtie's wrinkled hand resting on the top of the sheet. "I promise, Aunt Myrtie. Don't you worry about a thing. I'll take care of it all."

She smiled again at her aunt's expression of unbelief. Carrie had called Charlie before they'd left the farmhouse, so she knew he would take care of opening the restaurant in the morning until Carrie could get there to help. But the restaurant wasn't a priority with her right now. Her aunt was.

Half an hour later the nurses got Aunt Myrtle settled in a regular room upstairs and Carrie finally felt comfortable leaving her.

"I'll be back later to check on you, Aunt Myrtle. You just do what the nurses and doctor tells you and rest. That's an order," she added in her teacher voice.

As weariness swept over her, Carrie rode the elevator back down to the main floor of the hospital and walked down the carpeted hallway toward the main doors. She was so exhausted and there was so much to do.

As she passed the waiting room, she glanced through the doorway and came to a halt.

Neil.

She couldn't believe he'd stayed here and waited patiently all the time she was upstairs with her aunt. And worse, she couldn't believe she'd forgotten all about him. As she entered the waiting room, she saw his head come up. It looked like he had been praying.

"I'm so sorry, Neil. I thought you would have left by now." Carrie sat down in the chair next to him.

"Couldn't go anywhere until I knew Miss Myrtle was going to be okay, now could I? What did the doctor say?"

"She's been admitted. He thinks she has double pneumonia, but he's also going to run a bunch of tests on her heart." As she repeated what the doctor had told her, Carrie felt the fear sweep over her again. "I don't know what I would do if it's something serious. I'm so scared of something happening to her, Neil. Aunt Myrtle's always been there for me."

Neil reached over and placed his hand on hers, resting on her knee. "I've been praying ever since we got here with her. God has it all in control and I firmly believe she's going to be just fine now, so try not to worry. Okay?"

Carrie felt a sense of peace wash over her at the touch of Neil's hand on hers. It had been so long since she'd opened herself to contact from another person—especially a man—and it made her feel safe to know he was here beside her. How thankful she was he was with her.

Neil Johnston was one of the most loyal men she'd ever met, and had such integrity. He could have left the hospital hours ago and most men probably would have; but he hadn't left until he knew Myrtle was okay. Neil was a true friend.

"Thanks, Neil. It feels good to have a friend right now. I really appreciate you being there for us tonight to help me get Aunt Myrtle to the hospital. I wanted to call an ambulance, but she wouldn't have any part of that—and I wasn't sure how I was going to get her here by myself...."

He patted her hand again and then removed it, Carrie immediately feeling the loss of his touch.

"That's okay. I'm glad you called. After all, that's what friends are for."

∧∧∧∧∧∧

Carrie spent the next few days working at the restaurant almost non-stop. Charlie still ran the afternoon and evening shifts, but Carrie was in charge of scheduling hours, planning the daily specials, ordering food and supplies, payroll, advertising, paying the vendors, and making sure all the other little details of running a business were taken care. She prayed daily that she wasn't messing things up too badly. She was a schoolteacher, after all—not a business owner.

She didn't have any idea how her aunt did it all.

After Carrie's shift ended each day, she drove to the hospital to spend the rest of the day with her aunt, filling her in on the happenings at the restaurant. Fortunately, Aunt Myrtie had improved a little bit every day and was hopefully going to be released from the hospital in the next few days. The further testing they had done showed there was no damage to her heart, but the pneumonia had weakened her to the point it was going to take her a few weeks to get back on her feet again. That meant that at least for the time being, Carrie was going to have to continue to run *Meyers Place*. Aunt Myrtle kept apologizing for messing up Carrie's vacation by getting sick, but Carrie told her she was happy she was here to be able to help—which was true.

But the clock was ticking. Carrie only had three more weeks before she was going to have to head back to her job in the city and that worried her. She wasn't sure her aunt was going to be ready to go back to full-time work at the restaurant by then, but prayed that somehow God was going to work it all out for all of them. Carrie prayed and was comforted by the faith that God had everything under control which was a very good thing; because she certainly didn't feel like she did.

∧∧∧∧∧

Aunt Myrtle came home a few days later, some of her more normal spunk starting to show when she argued with Carrie about sleeping arrangements.

"I'm seventy-two years old and am perfectly capable of taking care of myself. You can go back to staying up in the cabin and I'll give you a call if I need you."

Carrie shook her head vehemently. "Like you called last time, right? Forget it, Aunt Myrtie. It's not gonna happen."

When the smile on her aunt's face turned sheepish, Carrie smiled back at her.

"I'm staying right here—with you, Aunt Myrtle. No arguments. I only have a few weeks left anyway before I have to go home, and I can't think of anywhere else I would rather spend them. I'll be at the restaurant in the mornings, and here with you in the afternoons and evenings. We can spend some time reminiscing about my childhood summers here. How does that sound?"

Carrie let out a sigh of relief when her aunt finally realized Carrie was just as stubborn as she was and gave in to Carrie's request. There were some mumblings about "young pipsqueaks think they know everything", and "don't know where she gets her stubbornness from", but eventually Carrie won the battle.

She drove up the hill to the cabin and packed all her belongings, cleaned the cabin as thoroughly as she could, and came back down the mountainside and unloaded her car. As she hauled box after box out of the car, she groaned. She was positive she hadn't had this much stuff when she came to Tennessee. Then she thought about the fact that she'd bought the printer/scanner since she'd come, and then, of course, there was the painting she'd purchased at Neil's, along with a few other souvenirs she'd found along her journey; plus there were the groceries from the cupboards and refrigerator. It seemed to take her forever to get everything unloaded from her car and put away, but it was good to know when it was all done that she didn't have to go back to get anything from the cabin before she left.

She took a few moments to stand in the cabin one last time before she closed and locked the door. As memories swept over her of her first night here, about how stressed she had been the first time she'd walked in the front door, she gave a sigh of relief. She'd come a long way since then. She said a quick prayer of thanks to God for bringing her there for the summer. Here on the side of this mountain, she'd been able to rest and recover, and had started the journey that had eventually led her back to her Lord and Savior.

Back at Aunt Myrtle's farmhouse, she set about getting her aunt comfortably settled. Fortunately, her aunt's bedroom was on the main floor, which made things much easier as the doctor had given her strict orders that she wasn't supposed to go up and down stairs for a few weeks. Carrie took the bedroom on the second floor that had always been hers during her summer visits. Seeing the flowery wallpaper and cheerful patchwork quilt on the bed brought back many happy memories for her.

This summer's visit certainly hadn't turned out exactly as she had planned with Aunt Myrtle's health issues, but she was just thankful she had been here to help out. And keeping busy at the restaurant had definitely helped her with her healing process. Her last session with Susan had resulted in a clean bill of health and clearance to return to her job teaching. Susan had given her a big hug at the end of their last session and had told her she would be praying for her and to keep in touch.

Her sessions with Susan had finally given her a real breakthrough. She had shared Lloyd Taylor's letter with her therapist, and had talked for hours about her memories of that terrible night and her remaining fears. After much consulting and much prayer—even though he hadn't come right out and asked for it in his letter to her—Carrie had been working on forgiving Lloyd Taylor for what he had done to her. There was a part of her that knew until she was able to completely forgive him, she would never be totally free from the trauma she had suffered under his hands. She had come a long way. The bad dreams had lessened in intensity, and for the first time in months she was able to go to sleep without leaving a light on. That was a definite improvement, and she hadn't had any flashbacks in over a month. But she wanted to be totally free from it.

She prayed about her situation every night, searching for and reading scriptures from the Bible about hope and not being fearful. Carrie was healing; it was obvious to her in the peace she now felt in her soul. She also continued to read what the Bible had to say about forgiveness. The Lord's Prayer in the book of Matthew stated that if she wasn't willing to forgive, she wouldn't receive forgiveness. It was so much easier said than done, but she was going to keep trying.

Carrie had also spent a great deal of time talking about her situation with Aunt Myrtle, respecting the older woman's mature wisdom. When Aunt Myrtle had heard about Lloyd Taylor's request, they had spent many hours praying together about it.

"None of us deserve God's grace, dearie. I certainly don't," Aunt Myrtle told her one evening as they sat at the table after their dinner.

Carrie looked at her aunt, not believing what she was hearing. Her Aunt Myrtle was one of the most forgiving, kind women she had ever known.

"How can you say that, Aunt Myrtie?"

The older woman shook her head and sighed as her eyes dropped to her hands clasped on the tabletop. "After your Uncle Jasper was killed in the auto accident..." Carrie saw her aunt struggle to get her emotions under control before she was finally able to continue. "I was so angry with God. And I was filled with hate at the person that hit Jasper's car and killed him. It took me many months of praying and reading the Bible before I was able to surrender once again to God's will and forgive the other man. But I have to tell you, it wasn't easy."

She reached across the table and took hold of Carrie's hand. "If you don't forgive this man, you are chaining yourself to the past. If you want to be free from what happened, really free, you have to take the steps needed to set yourself free. The only way you can do that is forgive him and let it go."

Carrie thought about what her aunt had told her and finally nodded. She was right. Maybe it was time to let go of the hate.

∧∧∧∧∧

While her mornings were spent at the restaurant, Carrie's late afternoons and evenings were spent in Aunt Myrtle's kitchen, working on harvesting, canning, and freezing the bushel baskets of produce that came out of Aunt Myrtle's vegetable garden. She was getting weary of picking the ripe vegetables and taking care of them all. But Aunt Myrtie was vehement about needing to take care of the food and not letting it go to waste. So, Carrie canned tomatoes, green beans, peas, carrots, and made jar after jar of Aunt Myrtle's dill pickles and bread and butter pickles.

"What are you going to do with all this food, Aunt Myrtie? There is no way you'll be able to eat all of this."

Her aunt sat across the table from her, slicing cucumbers for more pickles and just looked at her over the top of her eye glasses.

"So, I'll give it away. There are plenty of people around here who don't have enough to eat. I just know we can't let all that good food in the garden go to waste. That's not the way I was raised."

Carrie sighed, nodded her head, and went back to work snapping green beans. Of course, her aunt was correct—as usual. She just didn't know how she felt about being the one who had to do all the work. Then she mentally scolded herself for having such selfish feelings.

Then there were her feelings for Neil Johnston.

Ever since their connection at the lookout on the Foothills Parkway that day, Neil had pulled away from her. Oh, he was still very friendly and had been a huge help when Aunt Myrtle had become ill. He even stopped over several nights a week and brought Aunt Myrtle flowers or a little gift, like a book or a copy of a news article he thought she might enjoy. And sometimes Carrie would catch him staring at her with a look she couldn't quite decipher, then immediately look away as soon as he realized she'd noticed. She didn't want to admit it to anyone, but she missed spending time alone with him and she especially missed their talks. She had tried so hard to not care about him, but somewhere along the way, she had fallen in love with the quiet man. Unfortunately, it was obvious he didn't feel the same way about her.

She kept telling herself it didn't matter though; she was going home soon. But thinking of that apartment back in the city as home was getting more difficult every day she spent here.

∧∧∧∧∧∧

One weekend, Aunt Myrtle's two sons, Ralph and Walter, and their wives, came from Nashville. They had called their mother and checked on her frequently after she got sick, but had explained that neither of them had been able to get away from their jobs and commitments until now. If it had been her mother in the hospital, Carrie knew she would have been there immediately, and had difficulty understanding their reluctance to spent time with their mother, but then it wasn't her place to judge them.

The first evening together there was a huge family discussion around the dinner table about what they were going to do with their mother. Carrie sat quietly at one end of the table, flinching at the way they discussed Aunt Myrtie like she was some senile old lady. She kept wondering how she would act if this were one of her parents they were discussing. She knew someday she'd be faced with her mom and dad getting too old to live alone, and she wasn't looking forward to the decisions that would have to be made at that time.

Finally, Aunt Myrtle spoke up, and Carrie could tell by the tone of her voice she had had enough.

"I have sat here and listened to you four talk like I'm not even in the room, and I have not said a single word. But I've heard enough. Now, you are going to listen to me."

Carrie had to suppress a grin at the looks of shock that swept over her cousins' faces. It had evidently been a few years since they'd heard that tone of voice from their mother.

Aunt Myrtle had gained strength quickly in the past week or so, and Carrie was pleased to see the color of healthy rosy cheeks once again on her aged aunt's face. Tonight though, Carrie thought the heightened color was probably due more to her aunt's rising temper. She wondered if Aunt Myrtle's sons had any idea how angry their mother was at them.

"Since I got sick, I've had a great deal of time to think, and whether you boys think I'm capable of making my own decisions or not, I've made some. I don't know if you'll be happy with the decisions I've made, but when it comes right down to it, I don't really care."

Myrtle took a deep breath and then continued. "I've been blessed with excellent health for many years, but I've finally had to admit to myself that I'm not getting any younger." The elderly woman glared at her sons and daughters-in-law before softening her look.

"I knew this day would come eventually—when I would no longer be able to run the restaurant anymore, or take care of everything that needs to be taken care of." She looked across the table at Carrie. "I praise God every day that He sent Carrie here to help me out this summer. I don't know what I would have done if she hadn't been here—especially when I got sick."

Her voice faded away for a moment and Carrie watched her take a hankie out of her apron pocket to wipe her nose. "But," she spoke up again as Ralph's wife, Sandy, started to speak and she interrupted the younger woman before she had a chance to continue. "This idle time has given me plenty of time to think and plan. And this is what I'm going to do."

Carrie focused her attention on her aunt as did everyone else at the table. It was obvious Aunt Myrtle had made some decisions and Carrie really hoped her cousins were smart enough to not cause a family disagreement if they didn't like what those decisions were.

"For starters, I'm selling the restaurant," Aunt Myrtle stated. She looked over at Carrie. "I've already talked to Charlie. He actually approached me several months back before I got sick and told me if and when I was ready to retire from the business, he was interested. He's a smart young man, and I know he'll make a go of it. He's already been to the bank, secured a loan, and we're just waiting for the paperwork to process so we can have the closing."

Carrie looked at her aunt in surprise. All this had been going on under her nose and she hadn't been aware of any of it. She'd been at the restaurant every day for weeks working with Charlie, and he hadn't once given her a clue he was buying it.

Aunt Myrtle looked at her. "I asked Charlie not to say anything to you about it yet, dear. I wanted to be the one to tell you. I hope you're not upset with me."

Carrie quickly shook her head. "Not at all, Aunt Myrtie. You're right though. I think Charlie will be a great restaurant owner. He's already talked to me about some changes he wanted to implement and I hadn't done anything about it because I knew you weren't up to talking about it back then."

Her aunt nodded firmly. "Charlie will do fine."

The older woman turned back to face her sons. "Now, about the farm. I've already made the decision to sell it too. I've contacted a realtor and it's already been listed for a couple of weeks. As a matter of fact," Aunt Myrtle gave them all a little grin. "I've had a very generous offer from a young couple, and I've accepted it, subject to them getting their mortgage approved. I don't think there will be a problem with that though as they both have very good jobs, but we shall see."

Aunt Myrtie's oldest son, Ralph spoke up. "Mom, I can't believe you did all this without talking to us first."

When he saw a look cross his mother's face that Carrie recognized, he must have realized how his words sounded. Carrie tried not to chuckle as she saw him swallow hard before he continued.

"I mean, we're just concerned about you, Mom. Where will you live? Are you going to move into town now? Or do you want to move in with one of us?"

Carrie looked at her aunt, wondering what else the older woman had up her sleeve. She had a 'cat-that-swallowed-the-canary' look on her face.

"As a matter of fact, I've made several other phone calls and there's a nice retirement community near Nashville that looks like someplace I'd like to spend the last years of my life. For right now, I'll have a little apartment of my own, but when it gets to the point where I can't take care of myself anymore, I can move into one of the units where there is full-time nursing care. It'll be closer to you boys, yet I'll have my own place so I can still be independent, which—in case you youngsters didn't realize it—is very important to me."

The looks of shock on Ralph's and Walter's faces had to mirror what Carrie was feeling. Their mother had done all this from home while Carrie had been working at the restaurant? Carrie had a feeling they had all greatly underestimated Myrtle Meyers.

Her son, Walter, finally spoke up. "Mom, are you sure this is what you want to do? You and Dad built this place and lived here on this farm for years, and both Ralph and I were born here."

Aunt Myrtle slowly nodded her head. "I hear what you're saying, dear. But life changes and we have to be able to roll with the changes. As my recent illness reminded me, my health isn't going to get better. I'm not going to get younger, so I prefer to do what needs to be done myself—while I still have the mental capabilities to make the decisions that need to be made."

Carrie stood up from her seat and walked around the table to lean over and give her aunt a hug.

"Aunt Myrtle, I am so proud of you for doing all this on your own. You are awesome!"

Her aunt reached up with her hand and patted Carrie's arm, still around her. "Thank you, dearie. I'm just glad you were here when all this happened. It helped me have the courage to do what I did."

She gave her aunt a quizzical look, not understanding what her aunt was talking about, but was interrupted from asking any more about it when Walter's wife, Teresa, asked another question. The rest of the evening was spent talking more about Myrtle's plans. Carrie was glad Myrtle's sons were finally starting to take some interest in their mom's future, so she was more than willing to simply sit back and listen while they and their mom discussed her future.

∧∧∧∧∧∧

Before the weekend was over and Ralph and Sandy, and Walter and Teresa returned home to Nashville, Myrtle had marked items in the house she wanted to take to her new place. Her sons had also picked out items they wanted to have shipped to them. Myrtle had also made lists of those things she would either donate to a locate women's shelter or sell in the auction which was scheduled in a few weeks.

Before they left, Carrie gave each of her cousins copies of the book she had put together of their family history and Aunt Myrtle's memories of a simpler time. They and their wives had both thanked her, laughing as they looked through some of the old photos of them when they were younger and read stories of their childhood. It made Carrie feel good to know she'd been able to help them recapture some of their memories through the book—especially now that their mom was selling the farm. She also gave one to Aunt Myrtle, and had a copy set aside to take to her parents when she visited them in North Carolina before she went home.

She had actually made the decision to self-publish the book into a nice little paperback and was pleasantly surprised at how it had turned out. Carrie had originally planned to only purchase enough for her friends and family, but then at the last minute had purchased extra copies which she took to a couple of the nearby gift shops. Surprisingly, they eagerly agreed to have her sell them through their shops on a commission basis. She'd had a phone call just a week earlier, informing her one of the shops had sold out of the books and wanted more copies. Because of her trip to the mountains, Carrie had inadvertently discovered another career she hadn't even known existed for her. She was also thinking about compiling a broader-range book with more stories from other parts of the Smokies. But that was going to have to wait for another time. Her only thought right now were to ready herself to return to her life in Lexington.

∧∧∧∧∧∧

Aunt Myrtle pulled Carrie aside shortly after her sons' departure and asked her what, if anything, she wanted from either the house or the cabin. Carrie chose a couple of little things from the cabin, and then remembered her great-grandfather's Bible. She still had it in her upstairs bedroom upstairs, so promptly hurried up the staircase to get it. She brought it back down and handed it to her aunt.

"If it's okay with you, Aunt Myrtle, I'd really like to have this."

Aunt Myrtie took the book from her and opened it almost reverently, looking inside the cover at the inscription.

"Daddy's Bible," she said quietly. She lifted her tear-filled eyes to Carrie's and gave her a loving smile. "In his later years, it never left his side. I can remember him sitting on the front porch of that cabin up there with it in his lap. He read it every morning and evening, and often in between." She took a deep breath and nodded. "I think he would love for you to have it."

Aunt Myrtle handed it back to her and Carrie finally released a breath she hadn't realized she'd been holding.

"But how about everything here in this house? Don't you want anything else?"

Carrie shook her head. "Not really. I don't need the photos as I already scanned all them into my laptop. And I don't need any more furniture. Ashlynn's and my apartment is already stuffed full."

"How about the patchwork quilt on the bed you always slept in upstairs?" her aunt asked.

Carrie gave her aunt a hug and finally agreed to take the quilt. What her aunt didn't understand was, the things Carrie would take with her were the memories, and they meant so much more than any material things.

∧∧∧∧∧

Carrie's last few days in Tennessee flew by—much faster than she wanted. She spent as much time as she could trying to help her aunt sort and pack her belongings. She knew it had to be difficult for her aunt to leave the only home she'd ever known as an adult. Aunt Myrtle had raised her family here, and it had been where her children and grandchildren always came for visits and holiday dinners. Aunt Myrtle didn't say much about all the changes she faced, but Carrie knew it had to be bothering her. There were so many memories that had been made there, and it was going to be sad to leave—for all of them.

One day when Carrie and her aunt were sitting on the front porch in the swing, sipping lemonade, and taking a break from all the packing, Carrie finally raised the question to Aunt Myrtle about how she was handling the move. Her aunt gave her one of her no-nonsense answers—as always.

"Change is a part of life, dearie. I've seen so many changes in my life—the loss of my family home in the Cove, my parents' deaths, and then of course, losing Jasper when he was still a fairly young man. Then my boys grew up, married and moved away to raise their own families."

She sighed as she gazed toward the mountain ranges in the distance, and then looked over at Carrie with a loving smile on her face. "One thing is constant though. I know whatever I face, God is with me and will direct me where I'm to go and tell me what I'm supposed to do when I get there—as long as I ask Him. That is why I feel so at peace with these decisions I've made—I prayed about them before making them."

Carrie nodded, and then sighed. "I wish I was at peace with things that are happening in my life, Aunt Myrtle."

Her aunt stared over at her a moment before she replied. "I know it's not my business, Carrie, but if you aren't happy with where you are in your life and what you are doing, that could be a signal from God that you're supposed to be making some changes in your life too." She paused for a moment. "I'm assuming you're talking about having to go back to the city and your job." It was more of a statement than a question.

Carrie nodded. "I want to go back, and yet…I don't. I know, that doesn't make any sense." She glanced over at her aunt, then back out at the land around them. "I'm doing so much better mentally since I came here. Being here with you at the farm has been good for me, and I guess I just realized I won't have this place or you to come back to anymore. I'll really miss it, Aunt Myrtle. I'll miss you."

Her aunt reached across the swing and patted her hand. "I know. I'll miss this place too. But the memories we have of this farm will always be with us. Nothing can take those away, and the book you put together of the old pictures of the Cove and my memories—that is priceless, sweetie." She gave Carrie a little wink. "And you can always come and visit me at my new place, you know."

It was quiet between the two of them for a time as they both were lost in their own thoughts. Then Carrie was brought back to the present when her aunt spoke up again. "You know, Carrie, some of my best thinkin' was done while walking these woods and fields around us. Why don't you get out there and do some walking and talking to God? After all, He's the only one who can give you the answers you need."

Carrie thought about it for a moment and then nodded her head. It sounded like a great idea. When she was a youngster she used to wander around the farm constantly, enjoying nature and the wildflowers and trees around her.

She looked over at Myrtle and smiled. "Good idea, Aunt Myrtie. I think I'll make plans to do that."

∧∧∧∧∧

The next evening after their dinner, Carrie did exactly that. Carrying her great-grandfather's Bible and a big walking stick that Aunt Myrtle had told her she should take with her in case she came across any unexpected wildlife, Carrie took off down the dirt lane and through what used to be the back pasture. Some of the farm land was being rented and farmed by a neighbor, so she avoided those fields as she didn't want to do any damage to the plants. There was still plenty of open land though, and she strolled up and down the rolling hills and through the tall grasses, enjoying the sound of the birds singing, and the feeling of the warm sun on her back and shoulders.

She knew exactly where she was headed—a spot she remembered from her past summers. It was a special place she and Uncle Jasper had always gone to when they were taking their walks around the farm. As she climbed the ridge in front of her and came to the top, she sighed in pleasure at the scene before her. Below sat a little valley surrounded by wooded hills. There were several horses and some dairy cows in a fenced area, but other than that, it was wide open space. If she remembered correctly, when she used to come here with her uncle, the livestock had belonged to a neighbor on the other side of the woods. She was assuming that was still the case, so came to a halt, knowing this was the end of her aunt's property.

Carrie sat down in the tall grasses and closed her eyes for a moment, lifting her face to breath in the smells of the outdoors—moist rich soil, green growing things, and fresh mountain air. Aunt Myrtle was right. This was just what she needed. Here there was no one asking anything of her—no pressures, no expectations. It was just her and God.

And she had no more excuses to not talk with Him.

She so envied her aunt's relationship with God. Even though Carrie had made a decision back in her childhood to become a Christian and had been baptized, she had never had the type of personal relationship with God that Aunt Myrtle had. Maybe it came with age and wisdom—although she thought Neil Johnston had that type of relationship with God too.

So, what was different about them? What was she missing?

Her thoughts turned back to Pastor Gregory's sermon of the previous Sunday. She had felt like he was talking directly to her the entire time, and ever since, had felt restless and confused. He had preached on salvation, but had stressed that salvation wasn't achieved by simply saying a quick prayer to God. You needed to repent, be baptized, and be filled with the Holy Spirit. And in order to have the type of relationship like Paul had in the Bible, and like Aunt Myrtie had right now, it sounded like you needed to totally surrender your life to God and His will

Carrie sighed as she sat and looked out over the countryside. She certainly had never done that. As a matter of fact, after she left home and went to college, God's will for her life hadn't even been in her thoughts. She had been too busy finding her own way, enjoying her new-found freedom, and doing things the way she wanted.

A lot of good that had done her.

Maybe Aunt Myrtle was right. Perhaps what had happened to her had been a terrible thing, but as Carrie was well aware, it could have been so much worse. And if it hadn't happened, and if she hadn't been forced to, she never would had taken the time off work to come here. And if she hadn't come here to the mountains, she might never have come back to God.

She had so much for which to be thankful.

Carrie finally closed her eyes and started praying, a quiet whisper at first, then a little louder as she poured her heart and soul out to the creator of the universe. She told Him of her pain and her fears, her sins and her failings; she asked him to take over her life in every way, and as the tears rolled down her face, she even surrendered her love for Neil to Him. If God didn't feel he was the man for her, then she was going to have to accept that fact and let him go. She prayed for Neil's future and his happiness, knowing she was placing him in the arms of God, and there wasn't a better place to be.

As the sun lowered in the sky and the night mists started moving in, Carrie stood from her spot on the hillside, brushed the grass off her jeans, and headed back toward the farmhouse. Her mind was clear and her heart was at peace. She didn't need to worry about it all anymore. God would take care of her no matter what happened to her in the future.

While she made her way through the fields back to the farmhouse, a favorite verse from Philippians came to her: *Be careful for nothing; but in every thing by prayer and supplication with thanksgiving let your requests be made known unto God. And the peace of God, which passeth all understanding, shall keep your hearts and minds through Christ Jesus. Finally, brethren, whatsoever things are true, whatsoever things are honest, whatsoever things are just, whatsoever things are pure, whatsoever things are lovely, whatsoever things are of good report; if there be any virtue, and if there be any praise, think on these things.*

CHAPTER 14

It had been over a week since Neil had last seen Myrtle Meyers and Carrie at church. He'd spoken to them briefly after the service, and when Myrtle had asked him to lunch at her house, he had graciously declined, saying he had another commitment.

He had lied.

The truth was, he wanted to spend time with both her and Carrie—yet he was afraid to.

He'd already become way too attached to the two women. Now, Myrtle had told him she'd sold her restaurant and was just waiting for the final closing on her house and farm and was moving away. And all too soon, Carrie would be going back to her 'real' life in Kentucky, and neither of them would be around anymore. He had to learn to get along without seeing them and the best way to do that was to avoid being around them as much as he could now—before they disappeared from his life.

The toughest thing to do though would be to forget Carrie.

The shy and timid, almost melancholy young woman who had come to visit her aunt back in the spring had matured and blossomed here in the hills and mountains. Ever since she had shared with him her decision to forgive her attacker, it was as if she had finally been freed of the bonds of fear and sorrow that had haunted her eyes the first time he'd seen her in his gallery.

Now her eyes were filled with joy and peace, and when she smiled it was like a ray of sunlight in the room. He wanted to tell her to stay here—he yearned to be able to share what was in his heart and tell her he didn't want her to leave. But was his love enough for her? She had a life back in Lexington—friends and a job she was obviously good at and enjoyed. Carrie had told him countless times about her 'kids'—the students she taught—and how they touched her heart with all their little habits and sayings. It was obvious she loved each and every one of them.

She should marry some nice guy back there and have a family of her own. Yet whenever he thought about some other man winning her heart and having her love for the rest of his life, it sent a pain through Neil's heart that left him breathless. As much as he'd tried to deny it, what he felt for Carrie was far more than simple friendship. After four years of being sure God had meant for him to be alone for the rest of his life, he now felt perhaps there was someone who could fill the hole in his heart with her love.

Unfortunately, all she felt for him was friendship. She'd made that pretty clear. After he had kissed her, she had pulled away. Well, he was going to have to get over her— somehow.

Neil glanced up from the paperwork he was working on at the counter to see Patty Jackson, his part-time employee, enter the store. He had called her earlier and asked her if she could run the place for him for a few hours this morning. Now that she had arrived, he wondered if what he was about to do was a wise thing or if he was just setting himself up for a broken heart.

But he couldn't let her leave without seeing her just one more time.

He drove out the familiar road to Myrtle's farm, hoping he hadn't misjudged the time and missed her. Although if that were the case, he had to trust that was the way it was supposed to be. No matter what he wanted, God was still very much in control.

When he pulled his Jeep into the drive, he was relieved to see both Myrtle's and Carrie's cars still parked next to the old farmhouse. Carrie was just shutting the trunk of her car when he pulled in and parked next to her vehicle. He saw her turn and look to see who it was, and for a moment his heart lurched at what he hoped was a look of happiness when she recognized his Jeep. Then the expression disappeared and her normal friendly smile appeared in its place.

His heart feeling heavy, he got out of his car. Aunt Myrtle's dog, Buster, hurried over to greet him with a wag of his tail, then ran toward Aunt Myrtle who was just coming down the back steps.

Neil finally found his voice. "I was hoping I'd get here in time to say 'good morning' to my two favorite ladies."

Aunt Myrtle walked toward him and gave him a quick hug. "Good morning, dearie. What a nice surprise." He saw her look in Carrie's direction, then back at him. "I was hoping you'd make it before she left," she whispered to him.

He glanced at Myrtle in surprise, then saw her give him a quick wink before she turned toward her niece.

"I'm going to run back in and check one more time to make sure you didn't forget anything, Carrie. Don't you take off before I get back out here, you hear?"

Carrie smiled at her aunt and nodded, then glanced at Neil before she turned to lean over and arrange something in the back seat of her car. Neil walked over to stand directly behind her.

∧∧∧∧∧∧

Her heart was breaking. It was difficult enough to have Aunt Myrtle fussing over her all morning while she packed her car to leave, but now Neil was here, and her emotions were so fragile she didn't know if she was going to be able to hold it together. As she rearranged a couple of small boxes in the back seat, she took a deep breath. She could do this. Just a few more moments for good-byes, then she'd be on the road headed home to Lexington.

She stood back up and turned to find Neil standing right behind her. She caught her breath at his closeness and made the mistake of looking up into his face. His eyes burned into hers and she chewed on her lower lip at the intensity she saw there.

Carrie had really hoped he wouldn't come to see her off. Knowing he didn't care about her the way she felt about him was tearing her apart.

"Are you all packed? Is there anything I can do to help?" he asked her, his voice sounding husky.

She quickly shook her head and took a step back. "Nope. I think Aunt Myrtle and I have it all crammed in my car and I'm ready to go." She attempted a laugh, trying to keep the mood light. "Somehow I accumulated more stuff to take home than what I brought with me."

He gave her a little smile. "That usually happens when you go on vacation somewhere—and you were here quite a while."

Carrie nodded and glanced back at the house. What was taking her aunt so long?

Neil reached out and took hold her hand, and Carrie just barely stopped from gasping as she felt the familiar electricity run up her arm from his touch—directly to her heart.

"I am so glad I had the opportunity to meet you, Carrie Montgomery—to get to know you. It's been a pleasure."

She saw him swallow as his eyes continued to study her intently. "I do have to tell you, Carrie—I do care about you.

I really do. I'm just not sure I'm ready to have another relationship yet—especially a long distance one."

She felt the tears begin to build behind her eyes and blinked a couple of times to keep them at bay. Why now? Why did he have to bring this up now that she was leaving?

"It's okay, Neil. I understand. I know how much you still love your wife." She gulped to keep from letting the tears start. "I'm very glad I was able to meet you too, you know. You are a very talented artist. Thank you for showing me these beautiful mountains through your eyes."

Neil stared at her a little longer, still holding tightly to her hand. It almost seemed as if he wanted to say something more, but the moment was lost as they heard the back screen door slam. He dropped her hand, and Carrie's heart dropped to her toes. Whatever he'd been about to say, the moment had been lost.

The older woman hurried over toward where they were standing.

"Well, I checked every room in the house and I sure can't see where you've left anything behind, sweetie. I guess if I come across any of your belongings, I'll have to mail them to you."

"Thanks, Aunt Myrtle."

As the older woman came over and gave Carrie a hug, Neil stepped back to give them space for their good-byes. Aunt Myrtle sniffed a little as she pulled away from hugging her. "I sure will miss you, girl."

"I'll miss you too, Aunt Myrtle. Thank you so much for letting me come visit you this summer. It was just what I needed."

Carrie sniffed a little herself as her aunt stepped back and Carrie turned toward her car. There was no more stalling, no more excuses, no reason to procrastinate any longer.

It was time.

She glanced one more time toward Neil who stood stoically next to her aunt, his hands in his jeans pockets. He was standing there stiff-legged with an unreadable expression on his face as he watched her. She turned from him, got in the car and started it up, then gave a little wave through the open car window and pulled away.

She was really leaving and no one had done anything to stop her.

Oh, God. I will miss this place and these people so much. But I know every single thing that happens, happens for a reason. I also know You love me and have my best interest at heart. But this is going to be so hard, God. Even tougher than it was when I came here...Please help me. I'm going to need You more now than ever.

CHAPTER 15

Neil watched as Myrtle Meyers carefully wrapped various pieces of her good china and lovingly placed them in a cardboard box. It was Sunday afternoon and he'd been helping her do some final packing of those household goods she was taking with her. She'd invited him back to her house for lunch after church, but he'd been insistent that today she wasn't cooking and had driven them into Maryville to a nice restaurant so they could share what was likely to be their last meal together.

"So," she said after it had been silent between them for a few moments. "Tell me what you're thinking about, Neil. You've been quiet and somber looking all day."

Neil walked over to stand next to where she was working at the kitchen counter and reached up to pull another stack of dishes down from the upper shelves for her.

"Somber lookin', huh?"

Myrtle nodded. "Just tellin' ya what I see, boy."

He sighed and turned to lean back against the kitchen counter.

"What's eatin' you, Neil?"

Neil clenched and unclenched his jaw in exasperation. How could he tell Miss Myrtle what was bothering him when he couldn't figure it out himself? He'd made his choice. He'd let Carrie leave to go back to her life in the city without trying to do or say anything to change her mind. After all, he didn't want to have another relationship with a woman, right? That would just be setting himself up for another life of pain. Everyone he loved always left or was taken away from him.

"Guess I'm just wishing you didn't have to leave too."

The elderly woman glanced over at him, her eyes filled with compassion and love and Neil finally had to drop his eyes from hers to keep the tears behind his eyes from falling.

Too.

He'd said 'too'; it had just slipped out and he hoped she hadn't noticed, or if she did, that she wouldn't catch the significance of that tiny three-letter word.

No such luck.

He watched as Myrtle wrapped another teacup in newspaper. "She didn't want to leave, you know. It was terribly hard for her to go back," she finally said.

Neil sighed again, then felt himself being pushed toward a kitchen chair.

"Sit down, boy. I think we need to have us a little talk."

Myrtle took a seat in a chair across the table from him and Neil sat back in the kitchen chair and tried to ready himself for a lecture. He appreciated her wisdom, but there wasn't anything she was going to be able to say to him that would make him feel any better.

"Have you prayed about it, Neil?"

He lifted his right arm and ran his hand through his long wavy hair. He really needed to get a haircut. It had been a month or more since he'd visited the local barber and he was probably starting to look like a true mountain man. All he needed was a beard, and he already had a few whiskers started as he hadn't taken the time to shave the last few days either. He just didn't seem to have the motivation to do much of anything anymore. He hadn't even been able to do any painting since Carrie left.

"I've tried," he finally mumbled.

He heard her sigh. "Oh, Neil. There isn't anything you can't talk to God about. You know that." She chuckled, and he glanced over at her in surprise. She waved her right hand at him as if to scold him. "I'm right; don't you try to deny it."

Neil grimaced and then nodded. "I know. It's just...tearing me apart inside." He stood up, no longer able to sit still as the thoughts rolled around in his head.

"I really loved my wife. When she was killed...." Neil swallowed hard. "I thought my world had ended when she and our little girl both died. I decided right then I would never put myself into a position again where I could get hurt like that."

She nodded as if she understood. "So you chose to not fall in love again." She smiled at him. "So, how did that work out for you, Neil?"

Myrtle stood and walked over to where a small framed photo hung on the kitchen wall and took it down, running her gnarled fingers across the glass lovingly. "The first time I saw my Jasper, he was hauling logs for his uncle, up in the mountains. He was dirty and sweaty, but all I saw was the way his shirt tightened across his broad shoulders when he worked, and the twinkle in his big blue eyes when they turned on me. Then he winked at me, and I just knew."

She lifted her face to Neil's and he was amazed at the look of love on her face as she remembered. "I knew right then and there that he was the man God intended for me to marry."

She carried the photo back over and sat down at the table. "We didn't have as many years together as I would have liked. That car accident took him away from me way too early for my liking. So, I know exactly what you went through."

Neil gulped at the emotion he read on the elderly woman's face. She really did understand because she'd been through it too; and she'd never married again.

"But I wasn't as young as you are, Neil Johnston. And I never found any one I could love as much as I loved my Jasper." She turned her face up and looked him in the eyes. "You love my niece that way, don't you?"

Neil pushed the open palm of his hand across the rough whiskers on his face. He never should have started this conversation. He just wasn't ready for it.

"I don't know," he finally muttered.

"Well," Miss Myrtle stated in a firm voice. "You'd better decide if you love her or if you don't love her, because I feel God only gives you so many chances at a love of a lifetime. If you care about Carrie as much as I think you do, you won't let her go without telling her how you feel."

He turned his face to gaze unseeingly out the window, then looked back at her. "But what if she doesn't love me back?"

Neil heard her low chuckle. "I've seen the way her eyes light up whenever you come into the room. I've heard the tone of her voice when she talks about you." She smiled up at him. "If she doesn't love you, it's just because she hasn't figured it out yet. My guess is, she's trying to figure it out right now—just like you.

"So pray about it, Neil. Philippians 4:6 says, 'Be careful for nothing; but in every thing by prayer and supplication with thanksgiving let your requests be made known unto God.' So, talk to God and tell him your feelings and doubts, and then listen to what He tells you to do. He's the only one with the answers, Neil. The only one."

∧∧∧∧∧

"You wanted to see me, Neil?" Pastor Gregory asked, as he ushered Neil into his office at the church.

"Yes, thank you for making time for me, Pastor." He took the offered seat in front of Pastor Gregory's large wooden desk, and took a moment while he got settled in the chair to glance around the pastor's office. Two walls were lined with floor-to-ceiling bookshelves, jammed with large volumes of Bibles and what looked like other study materials having to do with the Bible. A couple of framed diplomas and certificates hung on a wall to the right of where Neil sat. This was the first time he'd been in the pastor's office and had felt funny about contacting him for a private consultation, but after his short talk with Myrtle Meyers, he knew he needed to talk with someone. He turned his attention back to the Pastor as the other man spoke again.

"What can I do for you, Neil? Is everything okay?"

Neil looked down at his clenched hands in his lap, then back up at the older man across the desk from him. "Not really." He cleared his throat. "As you know, I lost my wife and little daughter four years ago in a terrible auto accident."

Pastor's head nodded in understanding. "Yes, I'm very aware of your loss. You told me about it when you first moved here and started attending this church."

Neil felt the older man's eyes on his face, studying him carefully.

"Are you still struggling with the pain of that loss, Neil?"

Neil nervously cleared his throat again. 'His loss'; That didn't even begin to describe what he had been feeling when he'd left Chicago and moved here to lick his wounds and try to pick up the pieces of his shattered life.

"I've been here over three years now and I think I've settled in fairly well. My gallery has done quite well with both the local folks and the tourists supporting it."

Pastor nodded his head, a look on his face showing he clearly didn't understand where Neil was going with all this.

That was how Neil felt too. He really didn't know where he was headed with his train of thought either. Ever since he'd stood in Myrtle Meyer's driveway and watched Carrie Montgomery drive away, he'd felt like he was walking around in a fog. He couldn't concentrate on any one project at the studio long enough to accomplish anything.

"I guess what I'm trying to say is, I've been fairly content with my life here—even though I don't have a family—and I haven't really had any desire to have that type of a relationship again...until just recently."

Neil saw the pastor's eyebrows go up a little as if Neil's ramblings were finally starting to make some sense.

"I believe I'm finally starting to understand. You've met someone...."

"I did meet someone ... but she left." Neil squirmed in his chair, wondering how he could make the pastor understand all that had been going through his heart and his mind during his time with Carrie. "I didn't really know what to do about my feelings where she's concerned. I guess I'm scared to get too close to anyone again for fear of losing them. So I just let her leave. I never even told her how I felt because I was terrified of getting hurt again, and now she's gone and I don't know what to do about it."

"Hmmm." The older man continued to study him from his side of the desk.

"Do you have any idea how she feels about you?"

Neil released the breath he'd been holding in a huge sigh. "No. I don't. I'd like to think she feels the same way about me, but..." Neil hesitated, wondering how much he should share of Carrie's story, then finally decided if the pastor was going to totally understand the situation, he needed to hear it all. He knew Pastor Gregory had met Carrie this summer when she'd come to Sunday worship service, but he was certain she'd never shared with him about the attack. Neil didn't know if it was his place to tell her story or not, but if Pastor Gregory was going to give him an accurate observation of his situation, he needed to know the whole story.

After he finished telling about the physical attack on Carrie, Neil added. "Because she went through that much violence, I'm afraid it might have made her fearful of a future romantic relationship. We did become very good friends while she was here though, and I would like to believe she was attracted to me, but I never pursued it. I wasn't ready, and I was afraid to scare her away. Now I don't know what to do about my feelings for her."

Pastor Gregory nodded his head. "It is sad, the state our country has come to. Going through what she suffered—sometimes it completely affects an individual's ability to cope. Do you know if she's had therapy?"

Neil nodded. "She did—both in Lexington and also here during the summer. She was released to go back to work, so it must have helped." Neil couldn't help but feel it had been her time spent here in the mountains, reading and studying God's Word, that had finally given her hope. She'd seemed so much more at peace when she'd left.

The pastor leaned back in his chair and gazed at Neil for a moment before he spoke again. "My grandpa used to have a saying: 'Life is simpler if you plow around the stumps.'"

Neil just stared at the older man. He didn't have a clue what that statement was supposed to mean. Maybe the elderly Pastor Gregory was becoming senile. He blinked twice as he tried to decipher what he'd said.

Then the older man chuckled. "Let me state it a little clearer for you; you can always do the simpler thing—not become involved with someone who is obviously bruised and battered by her experience. It's easier. But that doesn't mean it's the right thing for you to do. You already know this, Neil, but let me remind you; even in the depths of your deepest depression, God hears your cries and because of that, you have reason for hope. He knows exactly what both you and Carrie have suffered.

"Let me ask you this. What would you do if she was still here and you had another opportunity to talk with her?"

Neil looked at the pastor in surprise as he replayed his words in his head. What would he do? Instead of avoiding her like he'd done before she left, he'd try and come up with things they could do together so he could spend as much time with her as possible. He wanted to know more about her—every little fact there was about Carrie Montgomery. And he would tell her that, if she would have him—damaged goods and all—he wanted to spend the rest of his life with her. He would woo her hand and hopefully win her.

But he'd missed his chance. She was in Kentucky now, and he was here. So, somehow he had to figure out a way to reach her long distance and let her know he was interested in her romantically, while still giving her a way out if she wasn't interested. It wasn't exactly something he could tell her over the phone.

"If she were still here, I'd let her know how I feel and tell her I want to spend the rest of my life with her."

"Well," Pastor Gregory said slowly, "if that's the way you feel, then you need to do something about it. After all, she may not know that's how you feel. And she never will unless you tell her."

∧∧∧∧∧∧

Carrie looked around her second grade classroom and felt a peace wash over her. She was finally ready for the new batch of students to arrive in less than a week when the school year started. Lesson plans were completed, bulletin boards were decorated, and the desks and bookshelves were arranged the way she wanted them. Right now it was very quiet in the room, but she knew when the children arrived, the room would come alive with chatter and giggles. She loved teaching, and it always made her heart feel good when one of her students finally had a new piece of knowledge sink in and their little eyes would light up with understanding.

She took a few moments to say a quick prayer for each of the young minds that would be coming her way in the near future. Her responsibility to teach these youngsters was a God-given gift, and not to be taken lightly. Her perspective on so many things had changed dramatically since her trip to the mountains and her re-kindled faith. She had wasted so much of her life in the last fifteen years, and was determined not to waste any more of it on the things of the world.

Looking around the room and not finding anything else that needed to be taken care of, Carrie headed home—back to the two bedroom apartment she shared with her friend, Ashlynn. At first it had seemed strange to come back to the city after her time spent in the mountains, but she was almost starting to feel like she belonged here again.

It didn't lessen the feelings of loss though for those she had left behind.

She put her key in the lock of the apartment door and swung it open while glancing through the stack of mail she'd taken out of the mailbox downstairs in the lobby. There were the normal bills and junk mail. Then her eyes fell on an envelope that was addressed to her in a handwriting she recognized and let out a squeal of glee as she shut the door with a bang.

Her roommate came running through the door from the kitchen. "Are you okay, Carrie? I heard you scream."

Carrie laughed as she handed her friend the rest of the mail, waving an envelope in the air. "Sorry, but I was so excited. I finally got a letter from my Aunt Myrtle. I've been waiting to hear from her so I would know she arrived at her new place in Nashville okay."

She ripped open the letter as she went into the living room area and plopped down in the nearest chair. Carrie had talked to her aunt on the phone a week earlier when the moving van had arrived and taken all her belongings to her new apartment, and Aunt Myrtle had sounded so excited on the phone, it had made Carrie wish she could have been there with her.

"So, what does she say?"

Carrie glanced up from the notepaper in her hands and then looked back down at her aunt's beautiful cursive handwriting. "She says she's getting settled in—really likes the new digs. There's a little screened-in porch off the back of her place and she has lots of shade trees, so she can sit there in the morning and have her coffee and read her Bible."

She quickly scanned down the letter, picking out the highlights. "Aunt Myrtle says she's going to a new church this coming Sunday as she's been invited by two neighbor ladies she's met. They've already gotten together for coffee at the facility's cafeteria a couple of times and are planning a shopping trip."

Carrie let out a sigh of relief. Her Aunt Myrtle was fine and was adjusting to her new life without any problems.

She stopped reading out loud and looked up at her roommate. "It sounds like she's doing great. I'm so happy for her. I wasn't real sure how well she'd do with such a big change, but it sounds like she's loving it."

She folded the letter and slipped it back in the envelope and stuck in her jeans pocket. She'd read the rest of it later.

It was such a huge relief to know her aunt was doing okay though. Carrie had been so worried about her.

Ashlynn spoke up. "Oh, by the way, there was another delivery for you."

Carrie looked up in surprise as her roommate pointed in the direction of their small dining room table. A huge bouquet of daisies in a beautiful bright blue vase sat in the center of it.

"You have to tell me who keeps sending you flowers, Carrie! Whoever he is, it must be serious."

Carrie gave a little groan. How could she explain it was serious—for her, but not for him. "I told you already. It's just a friend I made when I was in Tennessee."

Ashlynn snickered and stood up from her perch on the edge of chair, walking back in the direction of the kitchen. "Sounds like more than a friend to me. He's sent you flowers every week since you got home—and I'm assuming there's a card with each bouquet."

She nodded. Yes, there was a card with each one. But all that was on the card was a scripture reference and the words, "Praying for you." Not exactly words that spoke of romance.

"He's just giving me encouragement since he knew it was really hard for me to come back—and he knows everything I've been through."

Ashlynn stopped and turned to look back at her. "Everything?"

Carrie nodded. She hadn't held back any of the traumatic attack she had lived through, and had been quite blunt in sharing about her remaining fears. She had poured out her heart to him in a way she'd never done with another human being other than her therapists—let along a man. And what good had it done? She'd given the man her heart, but it had been obvious because of his willingness to let her leave that he wasn't interested in having it. He hadn't gotten over losing his wife, and it sounded like he never would.

So why did he keep sending her flowers?

Once Ashlynn left the room, Carrie walked over and plucked the little white envelope from the flower arrangement, taking the time to enjoy the beauty of the daisies. She had always loved the smiley faces of daisies. She had also enjoyed the other bouquets he had sent her last week and the week before. The first arrangement had been huge yellow lilies, very fragrant and extremely lovely. Then last week she'd received a beautiful bouquet of pink carnations. So, why was he sending her flowers every week?

She opened the envelope and pulled out the little card, already knowing there would be another Bible scripture printed on it, along with the words, "Praying for you—always." She appreciated knowing Neil's prayers were supporting her as she returned to her life here in the city, but she didn't know what to do about the flowers. She supposed she really needed to reply in some way and thank him, but she didn't know what the flowers meant, so wasn't sure how to respond.

Carrie took the little card and headed to her room to find her Bible and look up the most recent scripture reference. The first reference had been from Philippians, Chapter 1, verse 3: *I thank my God upon every remembrance of you, always in every prayer of mine for you..."*

The second scripture was from the book of Colossians, Chapter 1, verse 3: *We give thanks to God and the Father of our Lord Jesus Christ, praying always for you..."*

Now here was another scripture listed on the little card. She opened her Bible to I Thessalonians, Chapter 1, verse 2: *We give thanks to God always for you all, making mention of you in our prayers.*

Carrie smiled as she read the words so much like the previous scriptures Neil had sent her. He was praying for her. Even if he didn't love her the way she wished, it was a precious gift from God to know he was praying for her as a friend. It gave her comfort to know he hadn't just forgotten about her as soon as she drove away.

She just didn't understand why he was sending her the flowers. It had to be costing him a fortune. And how long was he going to continue to send them?

What did the flowers mean?

CHAPTER 16

The oil painting was finally starting to come together. Neil stood in front of a large canvas resting on an easel in his studio at the house. It was pouring down a cold rain outside, but inside it was bright and cheery with a warm fire snapping in the nearby stone fireplace.

He stepped back from the canvas and stared at it a moment, wondering what she would think of it? Well, it wouldn't be long before he'd find out. He still had one more thing to add to it and it would be finished.

Neil just hoped and prayed that when she saw it, she would understand what he was trying to tell her.

∧∧∧∧∧

Carrie's first full week of school had seemed like a very long one. Nineteen second graders were full of energy and questions and mischief. She had forgotten just how much trouble they could get into when given the opportunity. But all in all, it had been a good week and she felt good knowing she was finally starting to settle into her old life again.

Memories of the mountains continued to give her peace, and her daily devotions and time spent in prayer kept her centered on God's will, but for some unknown reason she felt like she was living in limbo. Ever since her return from Aunt Myrtle's, she'd felt like there was still something missing—like she was waiting for…something.

Reading her Bible daily helped anchor her. For the first time in her life, she felt God's love and peace in her life. And the terror she had felt for months was fading away. Reading the many verses in the holy book had reminded her not to be afraid, and that had surely helped.

She'd started going to a local church every Sunday, and had even become active in a Sunday school class for singles. There were several men in the class who had expressed an interest in seeing her outside the church activities, but so far Carrie had politely declined any of their invitations for dinner or a movie. She wasn't sure she was ready for something like that yet.

The memory of a tall, brown haired, brown-eyed man from the mountains was still too fresh in her mind.

Ashlynn wasn't home from her job at the school yet when Carrie arrived home that afternoon, so Carrie picked up the mail from their mailbox downstairs and headed up to the apartment in the complex's elevator. She had only been in the apartment for a few moments when the doorbell rang. Looking through the peek hole, Carrie saw a young man holding a huge flower arrangement of red roses. She gave her head a shake, chuckled, and opened the door.

Neil was consistent, that was for sure.

After the delivery man left with a smile and a 'have a good afternoon', Carrie closed the door and took the vase of lovely flowers into the kitchen. After putting the vase on the counter, she lowered her face to smell the beautiful aroma of fresh-cut red roses. She'd always loved roses and these were gorgeous.

Then she pulled the little envelope from the flowers and opened it. The verse shown was Philippians, Chapter 4, verse 13b. Carrie didn't even need to get her Bible to look this one up as it was one she had repeated over and over to herself in the days right after the attack:

Forgetting those things which are behind, and reaching forth unto those things which are before;

Why was this verse different than all the others? The previous ones had reminded her he was praying for her, but not this one. Was Neil trying to tell her to forget her past and move forward? She'd already done that, hadn't she, by forgiving the man who had attacked her and coming back to the city to pick up her life?

Or was Neil trying to tell her something else?

She looked at her cell phone sitting on the counter next to the vase and then reached out and picked it up. Should she call him? If nothing else, she should at least thank him for the prayers and all the flowers. It had been rude of her to not have thanked him weeks ago when the flower deliveries first started arriving. She just hadn't been sure what to say to him.

She still wasn't.

Carrie stared at the phone a few moments longer before finally finding his number in her phone listings and dialing it. Part of her was relieved when it went right to voicemail. As she listened to his deep voice asking the caller to leave a message and he'd call back as soon as he could, she felt a smile move across her face. Even if it was only a pre-recorded message, it was wonderful to hear the sound of his voice again. How she'd missed hearing it.

When the phone beeped for her message, she jumped, then stuttered as she tried to talk. "Neil, it's me…Carrie Montgomery. I just wanted to…say thank you for all the flowers and scriptures you've been sending me. I'm sorry I haven't called earlier, but wanted to tell you thank you. Hope you're well."

She sighed, not knowing what to say further. "Bye."

Carrie ended the call and sighed again. It was disappointing that she'd had to leave a message instead of getting to actually talk with him, but maybe it was better this way. That way he didn't feel obligated to talk to her. She put the phone back on the counter and leaned over again to take a deep sniff of the lovely roses. The fragrance was heavenly and the flowers were perfect, and they made her smile as she recalled all the happy times she'd had with Neil in Cades Cove. They'd had so much fun together, exploring the places of her childhood.

Forgetting those things which are behind, and reaching forth unto those things which are before;

She swallowed hard. If Neil was trying to tell her to forget him, it wasn't going to happen anytime soon.

∧∧∧∧∧∧

The next week, Carrie was disappointed more than she wanted to admit when days passed and no flowers arrived at their front door. She even snapped at her roommate sitting across the room when she mentioned it.

"I know he didn't send me any flowers, Ashlynn, you don't have to remind me. But it's okay, really. I'm sure the only reason he sent them earlier was to encourage me during my first weeks back at work. Now that I'm settled in, he probably doesn't feel it's necessary anymore, and that's fine with me. I'm fine," Carrie repeated, almost trying to convince herself more than Ashlynn.

Ashlynn gave her a look that was filled with sympathy. "I'm so sorry, sweetie."

Carrie waved her hands through the air as if to dismiss the topic and turned to leave the room. "No, honestly, it's okay."

Before she left the room she saw Ashlynn's look of pity again. Since Carrie's return to Lexington, Ashlynn and she had become even closer than ever. And because of Carrie's re-discovered faith, Ashlynn had also returned to attending church and reading her Bible. After talking about it several evenings, they had discovered they both had turned away from God when they'd left home and gone off to college. And they had become wise enough now to know that had been a huge mistake. They both needed God in their lives, now even more than ever.

"No it's not okay, Carrie. I know you really liked him, and after the way Sean treated you, I hate to see you get hurt again. Sometimes I just don't understand men!"

Carrie just shook her head as she walked away. Her throat was too full to even talk about it anymore.

They both turned in surprise as the doorbell rang, then Ashlynn jumped up to answer it. "Maybe it's a flower delivery," she called out as she raced across the living room.

Before she could stop it from doing so, Carrie's heart took a little leap. She was really going to have to get control of her feelings. She couldn't believe how much those flower deliveries had come to mean to her. It had been like a little bit of Neil had arrived with each delivery, and just to know he was still thinking about her had meant so much. . . .

When Ashlyn swung open the door, a man wearing a UPS uniform stood there with a large flat wooden crate propped up against his leg.

"I have a delivery for Carolyn Montgomery."

Carrie walked over to join Ashlynn at the door. "That's me."

She glanced from the package to the electronic device the delivery man handed her and quickly signed her name with the plastic pencil, then handed it back to him.

"Is it heavy?" she asked, wondering if she should have him bring it in the apartment.

He shook his head. "Not really. Just big."

Carrie thanked the delivery man and tugged the wooden crate, with the words "This Way Up" and "Fragile" on its sides, through the door and into the apartment. She looked at Ashlynn and shrugged.

"I have no idea," she said in answer to the question in her roommate's eyes.

They stood there staring at the crate for a few moments before finally discussing the best way to get it open. Then Ashlynn hurried out of the room before returning with a flat blade screwdriver in her hand. Between the two of them they managed to get the top off the crate where it was marked 'open here'.

The interior of the crate was lined with foam board, and inside was a flat object about 28 by 48 inches, wrapped in multiple layers of bubble wrap. The two of them carefully pulled the object out of the crate and carried it to the table where they cautiously removed the tape and unwrapped what looked to be something in a frame. When the final wrap was removed, the painting was upside down on the table, and Ashlynn helped Carrie gingerly turn it over.

Carrie gasped as a Neil Johnston original oil came into view.

"Wow," Ashlyn stated as they both stood and stared at it.

"It's the Carter Shields cabin in Cades Cove," Carrie's voice was almost a whisper as she gazed at the painting, her eyes slowly taking in every leaf, every tree. Looking at the beauty of the image, it felt like she was actually there. Neil had so much talent.

Ashlynn's excited voice brought her back to the present. "Hey! That looks like you, on the porch of the cabin!"

"What?" Carrie moved closer to the painting to look at it more intently, and caught her breath at what she saw.

Ashlyn was right. It did look like her standing on the cabin porch near the flat stone steps, her right hand resting on one of the posts of the cabin's front porch as she looked down the steps at a man.

"Neil," she whispered.

For there was only one other person in the painting. A man who looked exactly like Neil Johnston was down on one knee in front of the woman standing on the cabin porch as if he were asking her to marry him.

CHAPTER 16

Neil paced around his living room. He should have called her back right away. Once he'd received the voicemail from Carrie, he'd struggled with what to say to her. He'd been so excited about hearing her voice again that he hadn't returned her call right away. Besides that, he was trying to figure out what it meant that she'd called him after all this time. Then a day or two passed, and now he felt like he'd delayed too long.

So he'd prayed about what to do—for days. He'd taken two days away from both the studio and the house and had escaped to the mountains, driving around on back roads not frequented by tourists and taking lots of photos; but mostly he stopped and sat and looked out at the serenity of the mountains and prayed to God for wisdom so he would know what to do.

He continued to feel like he was supposed to wait, although he didn't know why.

Now he'd shipped the painting to her and was worried he should have delivered it in person instead. What if she didn't understand what he was trying to tell her in the painting? What if she'd found some handsome man in Lexington who had won her heart? For all he knew, her old boyfriend was back in the picture. Had Neil waited too long and missed his chance with her?

Finally after days of stewing and worrying about it until he couldn't get any work done, he prayed about it again and determined he needed to turn it back over to God—who was in charge of it all anyway. God already knew what was in their future, and Neil needed to have faith that because He was in control, whatever happened would be in the best interest of both of them.

But if she'd received the painting and he never heard from her again, he'd have his answer; and if that happened, he was afraid his heart would never recover.

∧∧∧∧∧∧

Carrie hit town about noon, stopping at the restaurant only long enough to grab a bite to eat to bolster her courage and to briefly see Charlie and the rest of the crew. As she headed back out the door, she made a promise to stop back and visit with them again when she had more time.

Right now she had only one destination in mind.

The gallery was open, but there were only a few cars in the parking lot. Hopefully that meant there wouldn't be a bunch of tourists inside so she could see Neil for the first time in almost two months by herself.

As she parked her car, she sent up a quick prayer for wisdom and God's will to be done, then got out of the car and walked down the sidewalk in the direction of the gallery. She tugged open the front door and entered the store, once again struck by the beauty and light of the interior. This time though, her eyes didn't go to the ceiling, nor did they drift to the huge painting on the opposite wall, but instead turned directly toward the counter to the right of the door. The young woman Carrie knew was Neil's part-time employee stood on the other side of the counter, instantly perking up at the sight of a prospective customer coming in the door.

"Good afternoon," she said with a distinctive Tennessee twang in her voice. "May I help you find something?"

Carrie walked toward the counter and smiled. "Yes, you may. I'm looking for Neil."

The young woman, who Carrie now remembered was named Patty, shook her head. "I'm sorry. Mr. Johnston isn't in the gallery today. But perhaps I can show you something. Was there a specific type of painting you wanted? Or are you more interested in some of Mr. Johnston's photography or sculptures...."

Carrie held in a laugh she could feel just under the surface. She was tempted for a moment to tell the young lady she already had the painting of her dreams sitting back in her apartment in Lexington, but she knew she was only trying to do the job Neil had hired her to do. And she was doing it very well. Carrie would have to tell Neil to give her a raise.

"I'm a friend of Neil's, Patty, and I really need to find him. It's very important. Do you know where he is today?"

The young woman's smile changed to more of a friendly one and she quickly nodded. "I'm sorry, ma'am. I didn't know you were a friend." She came from around the back of the counter. "He told me he was going to the Cove today, if that helps. I think he said he was going to do some drawings...."

Carrie raised her hand up to stop the young woman. She'd heard all she needed to hear. As she turned to leave, she took the time to call back over her shoulder. "Would you please phone him and tell him Carrie Montgomery is coming to the Cove to talk to him? Tell him he'll know where to find me."

"But how will he know? That's a big place!"

Carrie hurried out the door, Patty's words fading away as she let the door close behind her. She grabbed a jacket from the rear seat of her car and slipped it on before she got back in the driver's seat. It had clouded up on her drive south and without the sun to warm it, the air was starting to feel like late September.

She turned the car toward the Cove, her eyes soaking up the beauty of the scenery around her. In the higher elevation, the leaves had begun to turn and the mountainsides were starting to sport a kaleidoscope of colors. Having in the past only visited the mountains in the summer, this was a new experience for her. But she wasn't here to see the stunning autumn colors. She'd have time to look at the pretty leaves and colors later.

The drive down the Loop Road seemed to take her forever, even with little traffic. She drove the speed limit but had to fight the constant temptation to push down on the gas pedal a little harder. Maybe Patty had been wrong and Neil was really somewhere else. If that were the case, she might have a long wait, or maybe he wouldn't come looking for her at all. If that were the case, she didn't know what she'd do next.

Either way, she was going to the Carter Shields cabin and wait for him. Hopefully Neil would recognize the message she had left for him with Patty back at the gallery. She prayed he would understand what she was trying to say by coming here.

And she prayed he wouldn't let her down.

∧∧∧∧∧

A young woman Park Ranger by the name of Audrey sat with Carrie that afternoon as she waited at the Carter Shields cabin. In between visitors to the cabin, they perched on the front porch in the afternoon autumn sun, gazed out into the woods, and shared stories about the Cove—stories that had been passed down from both of their families. The other woman's great-grandparents had once lived in the Cove too and the more they talked, the more it sounded like their ancestors had been friends.

When all the other visitors had left and the evening mists began to creep into the valley, Ranger Audrey turned to Carrie.

"We'll have to leave soon, Carrie. I know you said you're waiting for someone, but the park closes at sunset."

Carrie nodded, a feeling of dejection rushing over her. Maybe she'd misunderstood the painting's meaning. Perhaps Neil had never received the message she'd left with Patty.

She had been so sure....

"Can't we wait just a little longer, please?" she asked, turning her eyes to look at Audrey and let out a sigh of relief as the other young woman reluctantly nodded her agreement.

Carrie had shared hers and Neil's story with the woman in the hopes she would allow her to wait as long as it took, but Carrie had really thought Neil would have been here by now...if he was coming. Maybe she'd misinterpreted the painting and what it meant. If that was the case, she was setting herself up for a huge heartache from which she would never recover.

No. She had to believe the message that painting had so clearly stated. She had to have faith that God was working everything out right now, just the way it was supposed to happen. She just needed to be patient.

Carrie once again turned her eyes back to the path leading from the parking lot. Every minute that passed made it a little darker so she couldn't see far, but she kept her eyes glued to the farthest spot on the path that was still visible. Ten minutes later she thought she saw the movement of someone or something walking down the path, but then wondered if she she'd stared at that spot for so long, her mind was just conjuring it up.

"Well, I'll be," she heard Audrey whisper next to her, then the woman grinned at her and stood from her spot where they'd been sitting on the porch. "I'll be around out back in case you need me, Carrie. I don't want to leave you totally alone, just in case." She grinned at Carrie again. "But make it fast. We're going to have to leave the Cove—soon!"

Carrie quietly thanked her and stood back up on the porch, her legs feeling shaky now that she could clearly recognize the figure walking briskly down the path.

It was Neil.

∧∧∧∧∧

Neil almost ran as he headed toward the cabin, his eyes straining through the gathering evening mists. Was that a woman standing on the porch? He prayed it was.

Oh, God. Please. Let Carrie be here like Patty told me she would be. Please don't let her have given up and left already.

He wished he'd received the message sooner, but had turned off his phone accidently and hadn't received the voicemail from Patty until about half an hour ago. As he'd been at the opposite end of the Cove, he'd had to drive out of the park and come all the way back in on the one-way road and precious time had been lost. His biggest fear had been she had already given up and left. Then he had seen her car still parked in the lot and had hurried to the cabin, praying all the way.

Please, Lord. Let this mean what I hope it means. She's here, so that has to mean she received the painting. Did she understand what I was trying to say by sending it to her, Lord? Did I make my intentions clear enough?

Neil approached the Carter Shields cabin, his steps slowing as he saw Carrie standing on the front porch—just like she had in his painting. And even though the evening mists and darkness was sweeping in around them, he could see well enough to tell she was looking at him with those big blue eyes and a huge smile on her face.

"Carrie," he finally choked out. Part of him felt like crying at the long-desired sight of her, another part felt like yelling out in relief.

She had really come.

He watched her step off the final stone step to stand on the path in front of him.

"Neil," her voice almost whispered. "The painting—it's beautiful. It's perfect." She smiled at him and he was close enough to her now he could see that in spite of the smile on her face, there were tears in her eyes. "I don't know what to say," she added quietly.

Neil took a deep breath. He'd waited so long for this day—this chance. He looked up into the treetops once for courage, then dropped to one knee in front of her.

"Say 'yes', Carrie. I love you so much and want to spend the rest of my life with you. I know we don't know each other as well as we should, but I'm willing to wait however long it takes until you're ready. Right now though, I need to know; will you marry me?" He pulled the ring he'd been carrying around in his pocket for over a month out of his pocket and handed it to her. "Please say yes."

He heard her gasp as she took the ring from him and glanced from his face to the ring, then back at him again. Neil knew the ring wasn't anything spectacular, but when he saw it in a jewelry store, he had instantly known it was the one he wanted to put on her finger. The diamond setting was small on the gold band, but would look perfect on her slim finger. He stood back up and waited nervously for her answer. He couldn't remember a time in his life when his happiness had rested so much on a single word. When he'd asked Lisa to marry him, he'd already known what the answer would be as they'd been dating seriously for over two years.

"Oh Neil," she finally squeaked out. "Yes, yes." She stepped closer to him and threw her arms around him, almost knocking him back to the ground.

"Yes, yes!"

She laughed and he finally felt like he could breathe again as an intense relief swept over him. She'd said yes.

He leaned down and took her face in both his hands, pulling her lips to his in a kiss, basking in the experience of the softness of her lips. For that brief moment in time, there was no one else in the world—just the two of them. As sweet as the kiss on the top of the mountain had been, this one was even sweeter.

She'd said yes!

The clearing of a throat brought him back to his senses and they broke apart to both look in the direction of their interruption.

He saw a blush sweep across Carrie's face, and then she grabbed his hand. "Oh, I forgot. Audrey, this is Neil Johnston, the man I told you about." She held up her left hand. "He asked me to marry him."

The young woman grinned as she looked at him and then back at Carrie. "No wonder you were determined to wait for him! I assume you said yes! Congratulations to both of you."

Then she pointed at the path toward the parking lot. "I really hate to break up this romantic moment, you two. But it's going to get very dark here very soon. It's time for us to leave."

The park ranger started down the gravel path with Neil and Carrie following her, holding each other's hands tightly until they got back to their respective cars. He gave Carrie another kiss before he finally released her so she could climb into her car.

"Where are you staying?" he asked. He didn't want to let her go, but because they had driven separate vehicles, he didn't have any choice.

She smiled up at him, and he could see so much love in her eyes, it almost took his breath away.

"I'm renting the cabin at Aunt Myrtie's old place. When I decided to come, I called the new owners of the farm and they said they'd love to rent it to me. It was almost like coming home—especially when Buster came running out to greet me. They adopted him from Aunt Myrtie, you know."

He nodded, then closed the car door and waited while she rolled down the window. "I'll see you there?" she asked, her voice a little shaky as if she was afraid to lose sight of him.

"You will," he stated. "I'll follow you the whole way." He gave her a smile, hoping there was enough light from the interior dome light of the car that she could see the love for her on his face. There was no way she was getting away from him again.

"I'll follow you anywhere, Carrie."

EPILOGUE

Carrie sat in the back seat of Ashlynn's car, smoothing her wedding gown the best she could, and feeling more than a little nervous—and excited. The long awaited day of hers and Neil's wedding had finally arrived.

She'd had a terrible time finding the perfect dress for this important day, but she'd finally found this one in a bridal shop in Lexington and had known instantly that it was the one. The dress was a one-shoulder neckline chiffon A-line dress, with a lace covered bodice that flared out from the seamless waistline to the long skirt. Carrie had wanted the dress as soon as she saw herself in the dressing room full-length mirror, but when she saw the look on her mom's face when Carrie showed it to her, she knew it was the one. With a simple wedding veil, it was perfect.

Ashlynn drove her car slowly down the Loop Road as they followed a long caravan of other cars who were also headed to the church where Carrie's and Neil's wedding was to be held. When Neil had suggested they get married in the Cove, the first place that came to Carrie's mind was the Primitive Baptist Church; the same church her grandparents and great-grandparents had attended and had been married in so many years earlier.

It hadn't been an easy task to make it all happen though because of all the stipulations in order to have a wedding in the Cove. They'd had to apply for a Special Use Permit which limited as to when they could have the service and how many people could attend. They'd also been informed there was no way to keep the normal visitors to the Cove from showing up at the church during the wedding, but Carrie wasn't worried about having strangers crash the wedding. It was a happy event and she wanted to share her special day with everyone who was interested enough to attend.

There hadn't been a normal wedding rehearsal for this wedding. After all, it was just going to be a small simple affair with only a few friends and family attending, and that was just fine with Carrie. She would have been content to be married by the local judge if that was what Neil had wanted, but he told her he wanted her to have a real wedding in a real church—albeit a smaller one than most women might want.

Ashlynn had tearfully agreed to be her maid of honor, hugging her and gushing about how she knew Neil was the one for Carrie from the very start. Neil had asked his brother, Carson, to be his best man, and Carson had quickly agreed, having already unofficially adopted Carrie as a sister.

Carrie had loved Neil's little brother from the start—a man equally as handsome, kind, and talented as his big brother, Carson Johnston was a CPA and lived in Chicago. He was married to a beautiful stay-at-home-mom named Meghann, and they had a sweet little boy about three years old by the name of Drew. Carrie adored Drew and loved spending time at Carson and Meghann's house. Carrie was hoping she and Neil would be able to have them come to their house for the Fourth of July weekend this year, along with Neil's dad and Carrie's parents. Carrie was so looking forward to having a real family get-together with *all* her family.

Neil had met Carrie's parents during a recent trip to North Carolina. They had all hit it off immediately, and Carrie had been thankful when her parents had told her they could see why she loved him so much.

God had truly blessed her.

But first she had to get through today's festivities. Following the ceremony, there would be a quiet reception at a rented hall in town. Then later, Neil and she were headed to Ashville, North Carolina on a week-long honeymoon. They'd made reservations at a lovely old Victorian bed and breakfast and were looking forward to site-seeing at places like The Biltmore. Afterwards, they planned to go to Lexington to get the last of Carrie's belongings to finish moving her into Neil's beautiful home—now her home.

Neil was going to continue to work on his art and photography and operate his store. Carrie planned to apply for a teaching position for the next school year. If she didn't get a full-time position, she hoped to at least get some jobs subbing. But they both knew, they'd make their plans and would have to wait and see what God sent their way. But no matter what came into their lives, they would be together to face the future.

Today was May 29th, and Carrie couldn't believe it had been almost a year since she and Neil had first met each other. So much had happened since that day in early May when Carrie had wandered into Neil's gallery and stared at the painting of the Carter Shields Cabin hanging on the wall. She hadn't had any idea of the significance of what that painting would eventually mean in both of their lives.

Back then she had been living a life of nightly terrors and mistrust of everyone around her. Her dreams had been haunted by evil, and she had never thought she would know the bliss of having perfect peace in her life—the peace that only came through a personal relationship with her Lord and savior. Never in her wildest dreams could she have imagined the significance of meeting Neil for the first time in front of one of his paintings of the Carter Shields cabin—especially when she thought about the second painting he had done of the same cabin. God had truly been good to them when he'd brought them together.

Who would have thought that something so evil, something so incredibly painful as the attack on her had been, would be for her good? If she had never been attacked and beaten by Lloyd Taylor, she never would have needed to come to the mountains for rest and healing. If she hadn't come here, she never would have met Neil and fallen in love with him. Her favorite verse from Jeremiah ran through her head again.

For I know the thoughts that I think toward you, saith the LORD, thoughts of peace, and not of evil, to give you an expected end.

The Lord had proven His thoughts for her were of peace and not evil. No one but God could have used something so terrible and turned it into a good thing for her.

She had also learned about her family history here in these hills--the steadfastness and faith of those who had come before her. And it was here she had learned about forgiveness. Her fragile heart had found healing in the majestic mountains that now surrounded her.

The cars ahead of theirs parked, and she and Ashlynn sat in their car for a few minutes and watched as the wedding attendees exited their vehicles and made their way up the wooden steps and into the old church. Carrie knew it would be darker inside the old building than it would have been in a modern church; but it was a bright and sunny day, so hopefully there would be enough light so they could all see the ceremony without any problem.

She and Ashlynn and several friends from Neil's church had decorated the old sanctuary this morning with pine boughs over the windows, and huge flower arrangements of yellow lilies, pink carnations, cheerful daisies, and red roses on the altar, and Carrie had a floral arrangement of those same flowers in her hands that she would carry with her as she walked down the aisle—all in remembrance of the many bouquets of flowers Neil had sent to her after she had first left Tennessee.

Her parents' car pulled in next to theirs and Carrie saw her mother get out of their car and walk briskly over to open her car door. She carefully helped her daughter out of the car and gave her a tearful hug.

"You look absolutely beautiful, sweetheart," her father said as he gently took her arm in his.

Carrie hugged her mom again and then hugged Ashlynn, trying not to cry and mess up her makeup. She'd waited so long for this day; she certainly didn't want to do anything to make it less than the perfect day she'd imagined. As her dad and she followed Ashlynn and her mother up the stairs to the church door, her dad looked over at her with tears in his eyes.

"You ready for this, sweet pea?"

She grinned at him as she heard the first few notes of the Pachelbel Canon being played by a violin, filtering through the open windows and door of the church.

"I'm ready, Daddy."

The two of them paused in the doorway before stepping into the church, allowing their eyes to adjust to the darker interior. She was surprised to see the small church was packed with people. Aunt Myrtle was there with her two sons and their wives. Neil had closed the gallery today so Patty could also attend, and Carrie could see her seated near the back of the church next to Charlie and his fiancé and the two gals from the restaurant. Charlie had told her he was closing for a few hours so they could all attend the big event. It also looked like there were many people there from their church family, and her eyes filled again with tears at the thought that all these loved ones had made an effort to be here and share this wonderful day with her and Neil.

After quickly scanning the crowded pews, Carrie's eyes turned to the front of the church where the old wooden altar stood. Pastor Gregory stood in the middle, and to one side of him stood the man for whom she had waited her whole life. As his eyes met hers, she sent up a silent prayer of thanks—for the good and the bad that had happened in her life that had brought her to this point.

She could hardly wait to see what God had in store for them next.

THE END

AUNT MYRTLE'S BREAD & BUTTER PICKLES

30 medium sized cucumbers (approximately 1 gallon sliced)
8 medium sized onions
2 large red or green peppers
½ cup salt
5 cups sugar
2 Tablespoons ground mustard
1 teaspoon turmeric
1 teaspoon celery seed
5 cups vinegar

Slice unpeeled cucumbers into thin slices.
Slice onions into thin rings.
Cut peppers into fine strips.
Dissolve salt in ice water and pour over the sliced vegetables.
Let stand three hours and drain.
Combine vinegar, sugar, and spices and bring to a boil.
Add drained vegetables and heat to boiling point.
Do not boil.
Pack into jars and seal.

Made in the USA
Charleston, SC
10 November 2014